Our Souls at Night

ALSO BY KENT HARUF

West of Last Chance
(with photographer Peter Brown)

Benediction

Eventide

Plainsong

Where You Once Belonged

The Tie That Binds

Kent Haruf

Our Souls at Night

PICADOR

First published in the United States 2015 by
Alfred A. Knopf, a division of Penguin Random House LLC,
New York, and distributed in Canada by Random House of Canada,
a division of Penguin Random House Ltd, Toronto.

First published in the UK 2015 by Picador
an imprint of Pan Macmillan
20 New Wharf Road, London N1 9RR
Associated companies throughout the world
www.panmacmillan.com

ISBN 978-1-4472-9935-6

3 5 7 9 8 6 4 2

A CIP catalogue record for this book is available from the British Library.

Printed and bound by CPI Group (UK) Ltd, Croydon, CR0 4YY

For Cathy

Our Souls at Night

1

And then there was the day when Addie Moore made a call on Louis Waters. It was an evening in May just before full dark.

They lived a block apart on Cedar Street in the oldest part of town with elm trees and hackberry and a single maple grown up along the curb and green lawns running back from the sidewalk to the two-story houses. It had been warm in the day but it had turned off cool now in the evening. She went along the sidewalk under the trees and turned in at Louis's house.

When Louis came to the door she said, Could I come in and talk to you about something?

They sat down in the living room. Can I get you something to drink? Some tea?

No thank you. I might not be here long enough to drink it. She looked around. Your house looks nice.

Diane always kept a nice house. I've tried a little bit.

It still looks nice, she said. I haven't been in here for years.

She looked out the windows at the side yard where the night was settling in and out into the kitchen where there was a light shining over the sink and counters. It all looked clean and orderly. He was watching her. She was a good-looking woman, he had always thought so. She'd had dark hair when she was younger, but it was white now and cut short. She was still shapely, only a little heavy at the waist and hips.

You probably wonder what I'm doing here, she said.

Well, I didn't think you came over to tell me my house looks nice.

No. I want to suggest something to you.

Oh?

Yes. A kind of proposal.

Okay.

Not marriage, she said.

I didn't think that either.

But it's a kind of marriage-like question. But I don't know if I can now. I'm getting cold feet. She laughed a little. That's sort of like marriage, isn't it.

What is?

Cold feet.

It can be.

Yes. Well, I'm just going to say it.

I'm listening, Louis said.

I wonder if you would consider coming to my house sometimes to sleep with me.

What? How do you mean?

I mean we're both alone. We've been by ourselves for too long. For years. I'm lonely. I think you might be too. I wonder if you would come and sleep in the night with me. And talk.

He stared at her, watching her, curious now, cautious.

You don't say anything. Have I taken your breath away? she said.

I guess you have.

I'm not talking about sex.

I wondered.

No, not sex. I'm not looking at it that way. I think I've lost any sexual impulse a long time ago. I'm talking about getting through the night. And lying warm in bed, companionably. Lying down in bed together and you staying the night. The nights are the worst. Don't you think?

Yes. I think so.

I end up taking pills to go to sleep and reading too late and then I feel groggy the next day. No use at all to myself or anybody else.

I've had that myself.

But I think I could sleep again if there were someone else in bed with me. Someone nice. The closeness of that. Talking in the night, in the dark. She waited. What do you think?

I don't know. When would you want to start?

Whenever you want to. If, she said, you want to. This week.

Let me think about it.

All right. But I want you to call me on the day you're coming if that happens. So I'll know to expect you.

All right.

I'll be waiting to hear from you.

What if I snore?

Then you'll snore, or you'll learn to quit.

He laughed. That would be a first.

She stood and went out and walked back home, and he stood at the door watching her, this medium-sized seventy-year-old woman with white hair walking away under the trees in the patches of light thrown out by the corner street lamp. What in the hell, he said. Now don't get ahead of yourself.

2

The next day Louis went to the barber on Main Street and had his hair cut short and neat, a kind of buzz cut, and asked the barber if he still shaved people and the barber said he did, so he got a shave too. Then he went home and called Addie and said, I'd like to come over tonight if that's still all right.

Yes, it is, she said. I'm glad.

He ate a light supper, just a sandwich and a glass of milk, he didn't want to feel heavy and laden in her bed, and then he took a long hot shower and scrubbed himself thoroughly. He trimmed his fingernails and toenails and at dark he went out the back door and walked up the back alley carrying a paper sack with his pajamas and toothbrush inside. It was dark in the alley and his feet made a rasping noise in the gravel. A light was showing in the house across the alley and he could see the woman in profile there at the sink in the kitchen. He went on into Addie Moore's backyard past the garage and the garden and knocked on the back door. He waited quite a while. A car drove by on the street out front, its headlights shining. He could hear the high school kids over on Main Street honking their horns at one another. Then the porch light came on above his head and the door opened.

What are you doing back here? Addie said.

I thought it would be less likely for people to see me.

I don't care about that. They'll know. Someone will see. Come by the front door out on the front sidewalk. I made up my mind I'm not going to pay attention to what people think. I've done that too long—all my life. I'm not going to live that way anymore. The alley makes it seem we're doing something wrong or something disgraceful, to be ashamed of.

I've been a schoolteacher in a little town too long, he said. That's what it is. But all right. I'll come by the front door the next time. If there is a next time.

Don't you think there will be? she said. Is this just a one-night stand?

I don't know. Maybe. Minus the sex part of that, of course. I don't know how this will go.

Don't you have any faith? she said.

In you, I do. I can have faith in you. I see that already. But I'm not sure I can be equal to you.

What are you talking about? How do you mean that?

In courage, he said. Willingness to risk.

Yes, but you're here.

That's right. I am.

Then you better come in. We don't have to stand out here all night. Even if it isn't something to be ashamed of.

He followed her across the back porch into the kitchen.

Let's have a drink first, she said.

That sounds like a good idea.

Do you drink wine?

A little.

But you prefer beer?

Yes.

I'll get beer for the next time. If there is a next time, she said.

He didn't know if she was kidding or not. If there is, he said.

Do you prefer white or red wine?

White, please.

She got a bottle out of the refrigerator and poured them each half a glass and they sat down at the kitchen table. What's in the paper sack? she said.

Pajamas.

That means you are ready to try this out for one time at least.

Yes. That's what it means.

They drank the wine. Do you want some more?

No, I don't think so. Could we look around the house?

You want me to show you the rooms and layout.

I'd just like to know more about where I am physically.

So you can sneak out if you need to, in the dark.

Well no, I wasn't thinking that.

She stood and he followed her into the dining room and the living room. Then she led him upstairs to the three bedrooms, the big room at the front of the house overlooking the street was hers. This is where we always slept, she said. Gene had the bedroom at the back and we used the other room as an office.

There was a bathroom down the hall and another one off the dining room downstairs. The bed in the room was king-sized with a light cotton spread over it.

What do you think? she said.

It's a bigger house than I thought. More rooms.

It's been a good house for us. I've been here forty-four years.

Two years after I moved back here with Diane.

A long time ago.

3

I think I'll just use the bathroom, she said.

While she was out of the room he looked at the pictures on her dresser and the ones hanging on the walls. Family pictures with Carl on their wedding day, on the church steps somewhere. The two of them in the mountains beside a creek. A little black and white dog. He knew Carl a little bit, a decent man, pretty calm, he sold crop insurance and other kinds of insurance to people all over Holt County twenty years ago, had been elected mayor of the town for two terms. Louis never knew him well. He was glad now that he hadn't. There were pictures of their son. Gene didn't look like either of them. A tall thin boy, very serious. And two pictures of their daughter as a young girl.

When she came back he said, I think I'll use the bathroom too. He went in and used the toilet and washed his hands scrupulously and squeezed out a little dollop of her toothpaste and brushed his teeth and then took off his shoes and clothes and got into his pajamas. He folded his clothes over his shoes and left them in the corner behind the door and went back to the bedroom. She had gotten into a nightgown and was in bed now, the bedside lamp alight on her side and the ceiling light switched off and the window open a few inches. There was a cool soft breeze. He stood beside the bed. She folded back the sheet and blanket.

Aren't you getting in?

I'm considering it.

He got into bed, staying on his side, and pulled the blanket up and lay back. He didn't say anything yet.

What are you thinking? she said. You're awfully quiet.

How strange this is. How new it is to be here. How uncertain I feel, and sort of nervous. I don't know what I'm thinking. A mess of things.

It is new, isn't it, she said. It's a good kind of new, I'd say. Would you?

I would.

What do you do before you sleep?

Oh, I watch the ten o'clock news and come to bed and read till I'm asleep. But I don't know if I'll be able to sleep tonight. I'm too keyed up.

I'm going to shut off the light, she said. We can still

talk. She turned in the bed and he looked at her bare smooth shoulders and her bright hair under the light.

Then it was dark with just the light from the street showing faintly in the room. They talked about trivial matters, getting acquainted a little, the minor routine events of town, the health of the old lady Ruth who lived in between their houses, the paving of Birch Street. Then they were quiet.

After a while he said, Are you still awake?

Yes.

You asked what I was thinking. One thing I was thinking: I'm glad I didn't know Carl very well.

Why?

I wouldn't feel as good as I do being here, if I did.

But I knew Diane pretty well.

An hour later she was asleep and breathing quietly. He was still awake. He had been watching her. He could see her face in the dim light. They hadn't touched once. At three in the morning he got up and went to the bathroom and came back and shut the window. A wind had come up.

At daybreak he rose and got dressed in the bathroom and looked again at Addie Moore in bed. She was awake now. I'll see you, he said.

Will you?

Yes.

He went out and walked home on the sidewalk past the neighboring houses and went inside and made coffee and ate some toast and eggs and went out and worked in his garden for a couple of hours and returned to the kitchen and ate an early lunch and slept heavily for two hours in the afternoon.

4

When he woke that afternoon he realized he was sick. He got up and drank some water and felt hot. He thought for a while and then decided to call her. On the phone he said, I just got up from a nap and I don't feel good, a pain in my stomach of some kind and also in my back. I'm sorry. I won't be coming over tonight.

I see, she said, and hung up.

He called his doctor's office and made an appointment for the next morning. He went to bed early and was sweaty in the night and couldn't sleep and in the morning he didn't feel like eating and at ten he went to see the doctor and was sent to the hospital for blood and urine tests. He waited there in the lobby until the lab had the results and then they admitted him with a urinary tract infection.

They gave him antibiotics and he slept most of the afternoon and again was awake much of the night.

In the morning he felt better and they told him he'd probably be released the next day. He ate breakfast and lunch and took a short nap and when he woke up around three she was sitting in the chair beside his bed. He looked at her.

You weren't kidding, she said.

Did you think I was?

I thought you were just saying you were sick. That you decided you didn't want to be with me at night.

I was afraid you were thinking that.

I thought it wasn't going to happen, she said.

I've been thinking of you all yesterday and last night and all day today, he said.

What were you thinking?

How you'd misinterpret my call. And how I could explain that I still want to come at night and be together. How I was feeling more interested in this than I'd felt about anything for a long time.

Why didn't you call me then? To tell me?

I thought it might even be worse, that it would sound all the more like I was making this up.

I wish you'd tried.

I should have. How did you find out I was in the hospital?

I was talking to Ruth next door this morning and she said, Did you hear about Louis? I said, What about him? He's in the hospital. What's wrong with him? They say he's got some kind of infection. Then I knew, she said.

I'm not going to lie to you, he said.

All right. Neither of us will. So will you come again?

As soon as I feel well and am sure I'm over this. It's good to see you, he said.

Thank you. You look pretty ragged right now.

I haven't had time to put on my face yet.

She laughed. I don't care, she said. That's not what I mean. I was just making a comment, an observation.

Well, you look pretty good to me, he said.

Did you call your daughter?

I told her not to worry. That I'd be out in a day and this was nothing to be concerned about. She won't have to take off work. I don't need her to come see me now. She lives in Colorado Springs.

I know.

She's a teacher like I was. Then he stopped talking. Do you want something to drink? I could call the nurse.

No. I'm going home now.

I'll call you after I'm home again and feeling all right.

Good, she said. I already bought some beer.

She left and he watched her walk out of the room

and he lay in the bed waiting to go back to sleep, but they brought his supper and he looked at the news while he ate and afterward shut off the TV and looked out the window and watched it turn dark outside out over the wide plain west of town.

OUR WORST NIGHT

5

The next afternoon he was released from the hospital.
But he must have been sicker than they thought, and
it took him almost a full week to feel himself again, to
feel well enough to call and ask her if it was all right to
come over that night.

Were you still sick?

Yes. I don't know what took me so long to get over it.

He showered and shaved and put on aftershave and
at dark took the paper sack with his pajamas and toothbrush and went out front past the neighbors' houses
and knocked at the door.

Addie came right away. Well. You're looking better.
Come in. Her hair was brushed back from her face and
she looked pretty.

They sat as before at the kitchen table and drank
and talked a little. Then she said, I'm ready to go up,
are you?

Yes.

She set their glasses in the sink and he followed her upstairs. He went to the bathroom and got into his pajamas and folded his clothes in the corner. She was in bed in her nightgown when he entered the bedroom. She drew back the covers and he lay down.

You didn't leave your pajamas here last time. That was another reason I didn't think you were coming back.

I thought it would look presumptuous. Like I was taking this for granted. We hadn't really even said much yet.

Well, you can leave your pajamas and toothbrush here from now on, she said.

It'll save wear and tear on paper sacks, he said.

Yes. Exactly. Do you have something in mind you want to talk about? she said. Not anything urgent. Just to start talking.

I'm full of questions, mostly.

I have some too, she said. But what are yours?

I wondered why you picked me. We don't really know each other very well.

Did you think I would just pick anyone? That I just want anybody to keep me warm at night? Just any old person to talk to?

I didn't think that. But I don't know why you picked me.

Are you sorry I did?

No. It's not that at all. I'm just curious. I wondered. Because I think you're a good man. A kind man.

I hope I am.

I think you are. And I've always sort of thought of you as someone I might be able to like and to talk to. How have you thought of me, if you ever have?

I've thought of you, he said.

In what way?

As a good-looking woman. Someone with substance. Character.

Why would you say that?

Because of how you live. How you managed your life after Carl died. That was a hard time for you, he said. That's what I mean. I know what it was like for me after my wife died, and I could see that you were doing better than I did. I admired that.

You never came over or made a point of saying anything, she said.

I didn't want to seem intrusive.

You wouldn't have. I was very lonely.

I assumed that. But still didn't do anything.

What else do you want to know?

Where you came from. Where you grew up. What you were like as a girl. What your parents were like. If you have brothers or sisters. How you met Carl. What's your relationship with your son. Why you moved to Holt. Who your friends are. What you believe. What party you vote for.

We're going to have a lot of fun talking, aren't we? she said. I want to know all that about you too.

We don't have to rush it, he said.

No, let's take our time.

She turned in bed and shut off the lamp and again he looked at her bright hair in the light and her bare shoulders, and then in the dark she took his hand and said goodnight and soon she was asleep. It was surprising to him, how quickly she could fall asleep.

6

The next day he worked in the yard in the morning and mowed the lawn and ate lunch and took a short nap and then went down to the bakery and drank coffee with a group of men he met with every other week. One of them a man he didn't particularly like. The man said, I wish I had your energy.

How's that?

To stay out all night and then still have enough left over to function the day after.

Louis looked at him for a while.

You know, he said, one of the things I always hear is how any story is safe with you. It goes right in your ears and out your mouth. I wouldn't want to get the name of a liar and a prevaricator in a little town the size of this one. A reputation like that would just about follow you everywhere.

The man stared at Louis. He looked around at the

other men sitting at the table. They were looking any-where but at him. He stood and walked out of the bak-ery onto Main Street.

I don't believe he paid for his coffee, one of the men said.

I'll take care of it, Louis said. I'll see you boys later. He went up to the counter and paid for the other's cof-fee and his own and walked outside and over to Cedar Street.

At home he went out to the garden and hoed for an hour, hard, almost violently, and then went inside and fried a hamburger and drank a glass of milk and afterward showered and shaved. At dark he went back to Addie's.

7

During the day she had cleaned her house thoroughly and had clean sheets on the bed upstairs and had bathed and eaten a sandwich for supper. As the day faded, she sat in the living room, quiet, motionless, thinking, waiting till Louis should come to the door and knock as it turned dark.

Finally he came and she let him in. She could see something was different. What's wrong? she said.

I'll tell you in a minute. Can we have a drink first?

Of course.

They went to the kitchen and she gave him a bottle of beer and poured wine for herself. She looked at him, waiting.

We're no secret anymore, he said. If we ever were.

How do you know? What happened?

You know Dorlan Becker.

He used to own the men's store.

Yes. He sold it and stayed in town. Everybody thought he'd move somewhere else. He never seemed to like it here. He goes down to Arizona for the winters.

What's that have to do with our secret being out?

He's one of the people I meet with at the bakery a couple times a month. Today he wanted to know how I had so much energy. Being out all night and then to do what I normally do in the daytime.

What did you say?

I told him he was getting the reputation of a gossip and a liar. I got mad. I didn't handle it right. I'm still mad about it.

I can tell.

I should've just ignored it and defused it. But I didn't. I didn't want them thinking anything bad about you.

Let it go, Louis. We knew from the start that people would find out. We talked about it.

Yes, but I wasn't thinking. I wasn't ready. I didn't want them making up a story about us. About you.

I appreciate that. But they can't hurt me. I'm going to enjoy our nights together. For as long as they last.

He looked at her. Why do you say it that way? You sound like I did the other day. Don't you think they'll last? For a good while?

I hope so, she said. I told you I don't want to live like that anymore—for other people, what they think, what they believe. I don't think it's the way to live. It isn't for me anyway.

All right. I wish I had your good sense. You're right, of course.

Are you over it now?

I'm getting there.

Do you want another beer?

No. But if you want more wine I'll sit here with you while you drink it. I'll just watch you.

8

I was raised in Lincoln, Nebraska, she said. We lived
out on the northeast side of town. We had a nice two-
story clapboard house. My father was a businessman
and did well and my mother was a very good house-
keeper and a good cook. It was a middle-class sort of
neighborhood, a working-class neighborhood. I had
one sister. We didn't get along. She was more active and
more outgoing, with a kind of gregarious nature that
I didn't have. I was quiet, bookish. After high school
I went to the university and lived at home and took
the bus downtown to my classes. I started off studying
French but switched to elementary school education.

Then I met Carl in my sophomore year and we
started dating and by the time I turned twenty I was
pregnant.

Were you scared?

Not of the baby. No. Not of having one. But I didn't

know how we would manage. Carl still had a year and a half to get his degree. On Christmas Day he joined me at my parents' house—he lived in Omaha—and together we both told my parents after dinner, all of us sitting in the living room. My mother just started crying. My father was angry. I thought you knew better. He stared at Carl. What in hell's wrong with you. Nothing's wrong with him, I said. It just happened. Well it didn't by God just happen. He made it happen. There were two of us involved, Daddy. Well my God, he said.

We got married in January and moved into a tiny dark apartment in downtown Lincoln and I got a temporary job clerking in a department store and we waited. The baby came one night in May. They wouldn't let Carl in the room. Then we took the baby home and were happy and very poor.

Didn't your parents help you?

Not much. Carl didn't want their help. Well, I didn't either.

That was your daughter, then. I didn't think she was that old.

Yes, that was Connie.

I only remember her vaguely. I know how she died.

Yes. Addie stopped talking and moved in the bed. I'll talk about that some other time. I'll just tell you now that when Carl graduated we both wanted to come to Colorado. We'd gone to Estes Park once for a short vacation and liked the mountains and needed to get out of Lincoln and away from everything. And start up somewhere new. Carl got a job selling insurance in Longmont and we lived there for a couple of years, then old Mr. Gorland here in Holt decided to retire and so we borrowed money and moved here and Carl took over his insurance office and his clients. And we've been here ever since. That was in 1970.

How was it that you got pregnant?

What do you mean? How does anybody get pregnant?

Well, my memory is we were all pretty careful and nervous back then.

But we were young too. Carl and I were in love. It's the old story. It was all new and exciting.

It must have been.

She let go of his hand and moved farther away and lay straight in bed. He turned and looked at her in the dim light.

Why are you acting like this? she said. What's the matter?

I don't know.

Are you asking about the circumstances?

I guess.

About the sex?

I'm being more stupid than usual. I just feel sort of jealous and I don't know what.

Out in the country on a dirt road in the back seat in the dark. Is that what you want to know?

I'd appreciate it if you would just call me a goddamn son of a bitch, Louis said. A man too foolish for words.

All right. You're a foolish son of a bitch.

Thank you, he said.

You're welcome. But you could ruin this. You know that. Is there anything else?

Did your parents ever get over it?

It turned out they actually liked Carl. My mother always thought of him as a dark-haired good-looking man. And my father could see that Carl was a hard worker and that he would take care of us. And of course he did. We had some hard times. But mostly as far as being financially comfortable after the first seven or eight years we were fine. Carl was a good provider.

Then sometime in there you had a little boy to go with the girl.

Gene. Connie was six then.

9

Addie drove her car into the alley behind her neighbor Ruth's house, got out and went up to the back door. The old lady was waiting, sitting in a chair on the porch. She was eighty-two years old. She stood up when Addie arrived and the two women came slowly down the steps, Ruth holding on to Addie's arm, and came out to the car and Addie helped her in and waited for her to arrange her thin legs and feet and then she fastened the seatbelt and shut the door. They drove to the grocery store on the highway at the southeast side of town. There were only a few cars in the parking lot, a slow summer's midmorning. They went in and Ruth held on to the shopping cart and they moved slowly through the aisles, looking, taking their time. She didn't want or need much, just cans or cartons of food, and a loaf of bread and a bag of little Hershey bars in foil. Aren't you going to get anything? she said.

No, Addie said. I shopped the other day. I'll just get some milk.

I shouldn't eat this chocolate but what difference does it make now. I'm going to eat whatever I want to.

She put canned soup and stew in her cart and boxes of frozen dinners and a couple of boxes of dry cereal and a quart of milk and some strawberry preserves.

Is that everything?

I believe so.

Don't you want some fruit?

I don't want fresh fruit. It'll just spoil. They went around to the canned fruit and she took down two cans of peaches in their sweet syrup and some canned pears, then a box of oatmeal cookies with raisins. At the cash register the clerk looked at the old lady and said, Did you find everything, Mrs. Joyce? Everything you wanted?

I didn't find me a good man. I didn't see one of them on the shelf. No, I couldn't find any good man back there.

Couldn't you? Well, sometimes they're closer to home than you think. She glanced quickly at Addie standing next to the old lady.

How much is it? Ruth said.

The clerk told her.

Your blouse has a spot on it, Ruth said. It's not clean. You shouldn't come to work dressed like that.

The clerk looked down. I don't see anything.

It's there.

She took her money from her old soft leather purse and slowly counted out the money in her hand and laid the bills and coins on the counter in neat order.

Then they went out to the car and Addie put the groceries in the back seat and got in.

Ruth was looking straight ahead at the highway, where the cars and cattle trucks and grain trucks were going by. Sometimes I hate this place, she said. Sometimes I wish I had gotten out of here when I could. These small-town small-minded pissants, she said.

You're talking about that clerk.

Her, yes, and everybody like her.

Do you know her?

She's one of the Coxes. Her mother was just the same. Thought she knew everybody's business. Had a mouth like this one. She makes me want to give her a good slap.

So you know about Louis and me, Addie said.

I get up early every morning. I can't sleep. And I sit out in the front room watching the sun come up over the houses across the street. I see Louis in the morning going home.

I knew somebody would see him. It doesn't matter.

I hope you're having a good time.

He's a good man. Don't you think?

I think so. But the returns aren't all in yet, either. He's always been kind to me, though, she said. He mows my lawn and shovels the snow on my walks in the winter. He started that before Diane died. But he's no saint. He's caused his share of pain. I could tell you about that. His wife could've told you.

I don't think that'll be necessary, Addie said.

That was a long time ago anyway, Ruth said. Years ago. I think his wife mostly got over it. People do.

10

Addie said, Tell me about the other woman.

Who do you mean?

The one you had an affair with.

You know about that?

Everybody does.

She was married, Louis said. Tamara. That was her
name. It still is if she's still alive. Her husband was a
nurse, working nights at the hospital here in town. It
was unusual for a man to be a nurse back then. People
didn't know what to make of it. They had a little girl
about four years old, a year older than Holly. A little
tough thin blond girl. Her father, Tamara's husband,
was a big sort of heavyset blond guy. He was a good
guy, really. He wanted to write stories. I guess he wrote
some at night at the hospital. They'd had some trouble
before and she'd had an affair with somebody back in

Ohio. She was a teacher in the high school like I was. I'd been there only two years when she got hired.

What did she teach?

She was one of the English teachers too. The freshmen and sophomore classes. Basic stuff.

You taught the upper-level courses.

Yes, I'd been there longer. Well, so she was unhappy at home and Diane and I weren't doing so well either.

Why not?

Because of me, mostly. But both of us too. We couldn't talk. We'd get in a fight or an argument and she'd start crying and leave the room and wouldn't finish what we were talking or fighting about. That made it worse.

Then at school one of you made some kind of a move, some gesture, Addie said.

Yes. She put her hand on my arm when we were alone in the teachers' break room. Are you going to say something to me? she said. Like what? I said. Like do you want to go out for a drink or something? I don't know, I said. Do you want me to? What do you think? That was in April, the middle of April. I was doing our taxes for the year and on the fifteenth, after supper I took the tax returns to the post office to get them mailed on time, and I drove by her house and I could see her sitting at the dining-room table grading papers, and so I parked down the street and came up on her porch and knocked and she came to the door. She was already in her bathrobe. Are you alone? I said.

Pamela's here but she's in bed already. Why don't you come in?

So I went in.

That's how it started?

Yes, on tax day. Sounds crazy, doesn't it.

I don't know. These things happen in all kinds of ways.

You know something about this.

I know something about how these things happen in people's lives.

Will you tell me?

Maybe. Someday. So what did you do?

I left Diane and Holly and moved in with her. Her husband moved out, stayed with a friend. And well, we got along for a couple of weeks. She was a beautiful hard wild woman, with long brown hair and brown eyes that were kind of like an animal's eyes in bed, and she had lovely skin, like satin. Her body was pretty thin.

You're still in love with her.

No. But I think I'm in love a little with the memory

of her. Of course it got bad in the end. One night her husband came over when we were eating supper in the kitchen. Tamara and her little girl and me. We sat there at the table talking with her husband like we were all advanced and sophisticated and that we were people who would just break up marriages and go on like free people. But I couldn't go on. I was sick of myself. Her husband there at the table and she and the little girl. I got up and left the house and drove out in the country, the stars were all shining and there were the farmlights and yardlights all looking blue in the dark. Everything looking normal, except nothing was normal anymore, everything was at some kind of cliff's edge, and late that night I came back. She was in bed reading. I can't do this, I said.

Are you leaving?

I have to. This is going to hurt too many people. It has already. And here I am trying to be a father to your daughter while my own is growing up without me. I have to go back because of her, if for no other reason.

When are you leaving?

This weekend.

Then come to bed now, she said. We have two more nights.

I remember those nights. How it was.

Don't tell me about them. I don't want to know.

No. I won't tell about them. When I was leaving I just cried. She did too.

Then what?

I went back to Diane and Holly and moved back in the house and lived downstairs and slept on the couch. Diane was pretty quiet about it. She was never vindictive or nasty or mean about any of it. She could see I felt like hell. And I don't think she wanted to lose me or lose the life we had.

Then in the summer one of my old college friends came out from Chicago and wanted to go fishing and I drove him up to the White Forest above Glenwood Springs, but he didn't like it, he wasn't used to the mountains. When I took him down a steep trail to a creek, he was afraid we were lost. We caught some nice fish too, but it didn't matter. We drove back to Holt and Diane met me at the door. Holly was sleeping, taking her afternoon nap, and we went to bed immediately, it just caught us that way, maybe the best time of any, that kind of unthinking urgency, while my friend was waiting for us downstairs to eat supper. And that was it.

You never saw her again?

I didn't. But she came back to Holt. She'd moved to Texas at the end of the school year and taken a job down there. Then she came back to Holt and called me. Diane took the call. She said, Someone wants to talk to you. Who is it? She didn't say anything, just handed me the phone.

It was her. Tamara. I'm here in town. Will you see me?

I can't. No. I can't do that.

You won't see me again?

I can't.

Diane was out in the kitchen listening. But it wasn't that. I'd made up my mind. I had to stay with her and our daughter.

Then what?

Tamara went back down to Texas and started teaching where she had accepted the job. And Diane let me stay.

Where is she now?

I don't know where she is. She and her husband never got back together. So there was that too. I don't like to think about my part in that. She was from back east. Massachusetts. Maybe she's back there.

You've never talked to her?

No.

I still think you're in love with her.

I'm not in love with her.

It sounds like you are.

I didn't treat her right.

No, you didn't.

I regret that.

What about Diane?

She never said much afterward. She was hurt and angry when it was starting. More then than later— more crying, I mean. I'm sure she felt rejected and mistreated. She had good reason to feel that way. And that was picked up by our little girl from her mother and probably is a part of her feeling now about men, including me. She has the feeling she has to be a certain way or she'll be abandoned. But I think I regret hurting Tamara more than I do hurting my wife. I failed my spirit or something. I missed some kind of call to be something more than a mediocre high school English teacher in a little dirt-blown town.

I've always heard you were a good teacher. People in town think so. You were a good teacher for Gene.

A good one, maybe. But not a great one. I know that.

11

You said you remember it, Addie said.

Some of it. This was in the summer, wasn't it?

August seventeenth. A clear blue hot summer day.

They were playing out in the front yard. Connie had
the hose running with an old-fashioned sprinkler head
screwed onto the end, the kind that sprays up a cone of
water, so they could run through it. She and Gene. He
was five years old then. She was eleven, still just young
enough to play with him. They had their swimming
suits on and ran back and forth through the sprinkler and jumped over it, screaming, and she grabbed
his hand and pulled him through it on his seat, and
held him over the water. I watched all that, then he
unscrewed the head and was chasing her around in the
yard, spraying her, they were yelling and laughing, and
I went back to the kitchen to check on dinner, I was

cooking some soup, then I heard a squeal of car tires and a terrible scream. I ran out to the front door, a man was standing out of his car, and Gene was crying, wailing, looking at the street in front of the man's car. I ran out. Connie was flung out in the street in her swimming suit, bleeding from her ears and mouth and the gash on her forehead, her legs wrenched up under her, her arms spread out at weird angles. Gene kept screaming and crying, the worst kind of desperate sound I'd ever heard.

The man who was driving the car—he's moved away now—kept saying, Oh God. Oh God. Oh God. Oh God.

You don't have to say any more, Louis said. You don't have to tell me. I remember now.

No. I'm going to say this. Somebody called the ambulance. I never did know who it was. They came and put her on a stretcher and I climbed in with them. Gene was still crying, I told him to get in with me. They didn't want that, but I said, Goddamn it, he's coming. Now go.

She had a terrible gash on her head, already swollen and dark, and blood kept running from her ears and mouth. They gave me towels to wipe at her. I held her bloody head in my lap and we drove, the terrible siren whining, and at the hospital they took her into the back entrance from the parking lot. The nurse said, In there, that way, but I don't think it's a good place for this little boy. I'll get somebody to take him to the waiting room. He started screaming again, the receptionist took him away and we went into the emergency room. They laid her down on the bed and the doctor came. She was still alive then. But she was unconscious. Her eyes were closed and she was having trouble breathing. One of her arms was broken and she had broken ribs. They didn't know what else yet. I told them to call Carl at his office.

I stayed with her. After a while Carl went home with Gene, to take care of him, and I stayed the night with her. About four in the morning she woke up for a few minutes and stared at me. I was crying and she just stared, she didn't speak, then she took a couple of breaths and that was all. She was just gone. I cradled her in my arms and rocked her and cried and cried. The nurse came in. I told her to tell Carl.

The rest of that day is a confusion of things. We arranged for her burial and in the evening we went to the funeral home. After she was embalmed we let Gene come in and see her. He didn't touch her. He was too afraid.

I don't know why he wouldn't be.

Yes. They'd put heavy makeup on her face to cover up the bad bruises and they'd closed the gash on her forehead and she was wearing one of her blue dresses. Two days later she was buried, I mean her body was buried, out at the cemetery. I sometimes feel I can still talk to her. Her spirit. Or her soul, if you want to say that. But she seems okay now. She once said to me, I'm all right. Don't worry. I want to believe that.

Of course, Louis said.

Carl wanted us to move to a different house in town but I said I wouldn't—I didn't want to leave this place. It was right out in front of this house. This is where she died, I said. This is sacred to me. So we didn't move. Maybe we should have, for Gene's sake.

He never got over it.

None of us has. But he was the one who caused her to run out in the street ahead of the car. He was just a little boy chasing his sister with a water hose. Afterward, your wife came over a number of times to check on me. That was kind of her. I appreciated it. I was grateful to her. Most people felt too uncomfortable to say anything at all.

I should've come with her.

That would have been good.

Sins of omission, Louis said.

You don't believe in sins.

I believe there are failures of character, like I said before. That's a sin.

Well, you're here now.

This is where I want to be now.

12

I won't be coming over here for a few days, Louis said.

Why won't you?

Holly's coming out for Memorial Day weekend. I think she wants to kick my butt.

What do you mean?

I think she's got wind of you and me. I think she wants me to behave.

What do you think about that?

Of behaving? I am behaving. I'm doing what I want and it isn't hurting anyone. And I hope it's good for you too.

It is.

I'll have to hear her out. But it won't change anything. I won't do any more what she wants me to than she does what I want her to do about the guys she goes out with. She keeps finding these guys who need propping up. They lean on her. She takes care of them for a year or so then she gets tired of it or something blows up and she's alone for a while. Then she finds another one to take care of. She's between guys right now.

Will you call me when you can come back?

13

The next day Holly drove out to Holt from Colorado Springs and Louis met her at the door and kissed her. They had supper sitting at the picnic bench in the backyard. And afterward they washed the dishes together and sat in the living room drinking wine.

I'm thinking of going to Italy for a couple of weeks this summer, she said. To Florence, for a class in printmaking.

I think you should. That sounds good.

I made the flight arrangements already. They've accepted me in a printing workshop.

Good for you. Do you need help paying for it?

No, Daddy. I'm all right. She looked at him for a moment. But I'm worried about you.

Oh? Is that so?

Yes. What are you doing with Addie Moore?

I'm having a good time.

What would Mom say?

I don't know, but I think your mom might understand. She was a lot more capable of forgiveness and understanding than people knew. She was wise, in many ways. She saw things in a bigger way than people do.

But, Daddy, it's not right. I didn't know you even cared for Addie Moore. Or even knew her that well.

You're right. I didn't. But that's the main point of this being a good time. Getting to know somebody well at this age. And finding out you like her and discovering you're not just all dried up after all.

It just seems embarrassing.

To whom? It's not to me.

But people know about you.

Of course they do. And I don't give a damn. Who told you? It must've been one of your tightass friends in town here.

It was Linda Rogers.

She would.

Well, she thought I should know.

And now you do. And you want me to stop, is that it? What good would that do? People would still know we'd been together.

But it wouldn't have to be the same thing. In your face every day.

You worry too much about people in this town.

Somebody has to.

I don't anymore. I've learned that.

From her?

Yes. From her.

But I never thought of her as being progressive or loose either.

It's not loose. That's ignorant.

What is it, then?

It's some kind of decision to be free. Even at our ages.

You're acting like a teenager.

I never acted like this as a teenager. I never dared anything. I did what I was supposed to. You've done too much of that yourself, if I can say so. I wish you would find somebody who's a self-starter. Somebody who would go to Italy with you and get up on a Saturday morning and take you up in the mountains and get snowed on and come home and be filled up with it all.

I hate it when you talk like this. Let me be, Daddy. I'll live my own life.

That goes for both of us. Can we make a pact on that? A peace.

I still think you should think about this.

I have, and I like it.

Hell, Daddy.

The next day a call came for Holly. She told Louis about it.

It was Julie Newcomb. Just like Linda Rogers, she had to tell me about you. I said I already knew. I said, But I'm glad you called. I was thinking about you the other day. I was out in a restaurant and ordered lamb. It made me wonder if your husband's still fucking sheep. She said, Fuck you, bitch, I was doing you a favor. Then she hung up.

That was pretty fast thinking on your part.

Oh, I never could stand her. But it's still embarrassing.

Well, honey, that'll have to be your problem, not mine. I told you, I'm not embarrassed. Neither is Addie Moore.

14

In the end I came to admire some of her qualities, Louis said. She was a good person, with a definite inner direction. She wouldn't do what others expected of her. We were pretty poor some of those years in the beginning, but she never wanted a career. She had her own ideas. She wanted her independence. I don't know if it made her happy, though. People talk about life being a journey now, so you could say that was what she was doing. She had a number of women friends here. They would get together at someone's house and talk about their lives and what women wanted. She talked about us, I'm sure. Women's liberation was just coming on big then. But we had some other problems too. And it was at least interesting to me that I would be taking care of Holly at night while her mother was at somebody else's house complaining to her friends about me. It seemed a little ironic. And there was that time with Tamara.

I thought you said she forgave that, Addie said.

I think she did. I think she wanted me back at the time. But I'm sure it came up in their talks. I could tell her friends thought differently about me. But she loved Holly. From the beginning. They were very close. Diane confided in her at an early age. I thought it wasn't right, talking to her that way, telling everything. But she did anyway. She kept Holly drawn in to her.

You haven't said how you met.

Oh. Well, we met like you say you and Carl did. We met in college in Fort Collins. We got married after we both graduated. She was a beautiful young woman. We didn't know anything about making a home or setting up a house. She'd never done any cooking growing up or much housework, her mother did all that. I grew up here in Holt.

Yes, I know that.

For a couple years after we graduated, I was teaching in a little school on the Front Range and when a job opened up in the high school here they hired me and I came back home and have been here ever since. Forty-seven years now. We had Holly, and as I say Diane didn't go to work when she might have after Holly started school.

I didn't really have a career either.

You worked. I know you did.

But not at a career like you've had. I was a secretary and receptionist in Carl's office for a year or so but we got on each other's nerves being together all day and then again at home at night. It was too much time together so I worked at the bank for a while and then in the city offices as a clerk. I'm sure you know that. It was the longest job I had. I saw and heard all kinds of things there. What people will do. What kind of trouble they get into. It was boring and tedious except for those stories you learned about people.

Well, Diane stayed herself anyway, Louis said. Throughout. As I say I can appreciate that now. I didn't then, at the time. But we didn't know anything in our twenties when we were first married. It was all just instinct and the patterns we'd grown up with.

15

On a night in June Louis said, I had an idea today. Do you want to hear it?

Of course.

Well, I told you about Dorlan Becker at the bakery who said something about us and I've told you about Holly's old high school friends calling her.

Yes, and I told you about going to the grocery store with Ruth and what the clerk said. And what Ruth said.

So here's my idea. Just to make a virtue out of a necessity. Let's go downtown in the middle of broad daylight and have lunch at the Holt Café, and walk right down Main Street and take our time and enjoy ourselves.

When do you want to do it?

This Saturday noon when they're the busiest at the café.

Okay. I'll be ready.

I'll call for you.

I might even put on something bright and flashy.

That's the ticket, Louis said. I might wear a red shirt.

On Saturday he came to her house a little before noon and she came out in a yellow bare-backed summer dress and he had on a red and green western short-sleeved shirt, and they walked from Cedar over to Main Street and down the sidewalk four blocks and then past the stores on that side of the street, the bank and the shoe store and the jewelry shop and the department store, walking along all the old-fashioned false storefronts. They stood at the corner of Second and Main in the bright noon sun waiting for the light to change and looked straight back at the people they met and greeted them and nodded and she had her arm entwined with his and then they walked across the street to the Holt Café where he opened the door for her and followed her inside. They stood waiting to be seated. People inside looked at them. They knew about half of those sitting in the café, or at least knew who they were.

The girl came and said, Is it the two of you?

It is, Louis said. We'd like one of those tables out in the middle.

They followed her to a table and Louis pulled out the chair for Addie and then sat next to her, not across from her but close beside her. The girl took their order and Louis held Addie's hand out on the table and looked around the room. The food came and they began to eat.

Doesn't seem too revolutionary so far, Louis said.

No. People are polite enough in public. Nobody wants to make a public fuss. And I think we're over-reacting anyway. People have more on their minds than worrying about us.

Before they were finished eating, three women stopped by the table individually and said hello and then went on out.

The last woman said, I've been hearing about you two.

What have you heard? Addie said.

Oh, how you're seeing each other. I wish I could do that.

Why can't you?

I don't know anybody. I'd be too afraid anyway.

You might surprise yourself.

Oh, no. I couldn't do it. Not at my age.

They ate slowly and then ordered dessert, in no rush at all. Afterward they rose and went out onto Main Street again and now walked back up the opposite side and past the stores there and the people looking out from inside beyond the open doors, open for any breeze there might be, and went over three blocks to Cedar.

Addie said, Do you want to come in?

No. But I'll be here tonight.

16

Addie Moore had a grandson named Jamie who was just turning six. In the early summer the trouble between his parents got worse. There were bad arguments in the kitchen and bedroom, accusations and recriminations, her tears and his shouts. They finally separated on a trial basis and she went off to California to stay with a friend, leaving Jamie with his father. He called Addie and told her what happened, that his wife had quit her job as a hairdresser and had gone out to the West Coast.

What's wrong? Addie said. What's this about?

We can't get along. She won't meet halfway on anything.

When did she leave?

Two days ago. I don't know what to do.

What about Jamie?

That's why I called. Could he come out and stay with you for a while?

When is Beverly coming back?

I don't know if she is coming back.

She's not just going to leave her son, is she?

Mom, I don't know, I can't say what she'll do. And there's something else I haven't told you yet. I've only got till the end of the month. I've got to close the store.

Why? What happened there?

It's the economy, Mom, it's not me. Nobody wants to buy new furniture now. I need your help.

When do you want to bring him to me?

This weekend. I'll manage till then.

All right. But you know how hard this is for little children.

What else am I going to do?

That night when Louis came to her house she told him about the new arrangement.

I guess that's the end of us, he said.

Oh, I won't think that, Addie said. Just wait for him to be here a day or two, will you, then come over to meet him during the day and then come again at night. We can at least see how it goes. I'll need your help with him anyway. If you're willing.

It's been a long time since I've been around little kids, Louis said.

Me too, she said.

What's wrong with his parents? What's their particular trouble?

He's too controlling, too protective, and she's had enough of it. She's angry and wants to do things on her own. It's not a new story. Gene doesn't put it like that, of course.

Some of his problems have to do with what happened to his sister, I take it.

I'm sure they do. I can't tell about Beverly. I've never gotten close to her. I don't think she wants that with me. There's something else too. He's losing his store. He's had this idea of selling unpainted furniture, people buy it cheaply and paint it themselves. I don't think it was ever a very good idea. He might have to declare bankruptcy. He told me that this morning. I'll have to support him till he finds something new. I've helped him before. I've agreed to help him again.

What is it he wants to do?

He's always been in sales of some kind.

That doesn't seem to fit him, as I remember him.

No. He's not the salesman type. I think he's afraid now. He won't say so.

But this could be a chance for him to break out.

Break the pattern. Like his mother has. Like you've done.

He won't, though. He's got his life all screwed down tight. Now he needs help and I'm sure he hates it. He's got a bad temper and it comes out at times like this. He never learned how to meet the public and he resents having to ask me for anything.

On Saturday morning Gene brought the boy to Addie's house and stayed for lunch and brought in his suitcase and toys and hugged him and Jamie cried when his father went back out to the car. Addie wrapped her arms around him when he tried to pull away and held him and let him cry and after the car left she persuaded him to come back into the house. She got him interested in helping mix up the batter for cupcakes and fill the paper cups and put them in the oven. Afterward they frosted them and the boy ate one and had a glass of milk.

I have a neighbor I want to take a couple of these to. Will you pick out two and we'll go by his house?

Where does he live?

In the next block.

Which ones should I pick?

Whichever you want.

He chose two of the least frosted and Addie put them in a plastic carton and they went down the block and knocked on Louis's door. When he came Addie said, This is my grandson, Jamie Moore. We brought you something.

Do you want to come in?

Just for a minute.

They sat on the porch and looked out at the street, the houses all quiet across the way, the trees, the occasional car that went by. Louis asked Jamie about school but he didn't want to talk and after a little while Addie took him back home. She made supper and he played with his mobile phone and then she took him upstairs and said, This was your dad's bedroom when he was a boy. She helped him put his clothes away and he went in the bathroom and brushed his teeth. He came back and lay down and she read to him for a while and shut off the light. She kissed him and said, I'll be right across the hall if you need something.

Will you leave the light on?

I'll switch on this bedside lamp.

And leave the door open, Grandma.

You'll be just fine, honey. I'm here.

She went to her room and got changed for bed and looked in at him. He was still awake, staring at the doorway.

Are you okay?

He was playing with the phone again.

I think you should put that away and go to sleep now.

In a minute.

No. I want you to do it now. She came over to the bed and took the phone and set it on the dresser. Go to sleep now, honey. Shut your eyes. She sat on the edge of the bed and caressed his forehead and cheek, and sat there a long time.

In the night she woke when he came into her bedroom. He was crying and she took him into bed with her and held him and eventually he went to sleep again. In the morning he was still with her in the big bed.

She kissed him. I'm going into the bathroom. I'll be back in a minute. When she came out he was standing in the hallway in front of the door. Honey, don't be afraid. I'm not going anywhere. I'm not about to leave you. I'm right here.

17

The second night was much like the first. They ate supper and she found a deck of cards and taught him a game at the kitchen table and then they went upstairs, where the boy got ready for bed and she sat down in a chair next to him and took his phone away and read to him for an hour and kissed him, leaving the light on and the door open, and went to her room and read. She got up once to check in on him and he was asleep with his phone still on the dresser. In the night he came as before into her dark room crying and she took him into her bed and in the morning he was still asleep when she woke. They had breakfast downstairs and went outside. She showed him around the yard pointing out the flowerbeds and naming the trees and bushes and took him out to the garage where her car was parked and showed him the tool bench Carl had used to repair things and the tools hanging above it on a pegboard. The boy wasn't much interested.

Then Louis came to see them. I wonder if you want to come over to my house with your grandmother, he said. I want to show you something.

In the backyard there was a nest of just-born mice he had found that morning back in the corner of the toolshed. The babies were all pink and still blind, squirming and moiling around and making little whimpers. The boy was a little afraid of them.

They won't hurt you, Louis said. They can't hurt anything. They're just babies. They're still nursing. She hasn't weaned them yet. Do you know what that means?

No.

It means when she stops giving them her milk and they have to learn to eat other things.

What will they eat then?

Seeds and bits of food she finds. We can watch them every day and see how they change. Now we better put the lid back so they don't get cold or scared. This is all the excitement they need for one day.

They moved out of the shed and Addie said, Do you need any help in your garden today?

I could always use a good hand here.

Maybe Jamie could help you.

Well, let's ask him. You willing to help me a little?

Doing what?

Pulling some weeds and watering.

Is it all right with you, Grandma?

Yes. You stay with Louis and he'll bring you home when you're through and we'll all have some lunch together.

The boy had never pulled weeds before. Louis had to point out what he wanted in the rows and what he didn't want. They did a little of that but the boy didn't care for it so after a while Louis got the hose and turned the nozzle on low and showed him how to water along the base of the plants—the carrots and beets and radishes—without exposing the roots. He liked that better. Then they shut the water off and went over to Addie's house. They washed up in the bathroom off the dining room. She had the food on the table and they sat down to sandwiches and chips and glasses of lemonade.

Can I play with my phone now?

Yes, then I want us to lie down for a little while.

The boy went up to his room and got his phone and lay on the bed.

Louis said, I still better not come over yet tonight.

Probably not. Maybe tomorrow. This morning went pretty well, don't you think?

Seemed all right to me. But I don't know what's going on in that little boy's mind. It can't be easy being away from home.

We'll see what happens tomorrow.

At night after he'd lain awake for a while he climbed out of bed and got his phone and called his mother in California. She didn't answer. He left a message. Mom, where are you? When are you coming back? I'm at Grandma's. I want to come where you are. Call me, Mom.

He hung up and called his father. Gene answered after the boy had begun to leave a message.

Jamie, is that you?

Dad, when are you coming to get me?

Why? What's wrong?

I want to be with you.

You need to stay with Grandma for a while. I have to be gone every day. You remember we talked about that.

I want to come home.

You can't right now. Later, when school starts.

That's too long.

It'll get better. Aren't you having any fun? What did you do today?

Nothing.

Didn't you do anything?

We saw some baby mice.

Where was that?

At Louis's house.

Louis Waters. You went over there?

In his shed. They were just babies. They don't have their eyes open.

Don't touch them.

I didn't.

Did you go over there with Grandma?

Yes. Then we ate lunch.

That all sounds pretty good.

But I want to be with you.

I know. This won't be for long.

Mom didn't answer her phone.

You called her?

Yes.

When?

Just now.

It's late now. She probably was asleep.

But you answered.

But I was asleep myself. I woke up when I heard the phone.

Maybe Mom was out somewhere with somebody.

Maybe so. Now you need to shut off your phone and go to sleep. I'll talk to you soon.

Tomorrow.

Yes, tomorrow. Goodnight.

He hung up and put his phone back on the dresser where Addie had set it. But later in the night he woke afraid and began to cry and went into her room.

18

He slept part of that night with Addie again. In the
morning they ate breakfast and then he went over by
himself to Louis's house and knocked on the front door.

Here you are again, Louis said. Where's your grandmother?

She told me I could come over to see you. She said to
say come to her house for lunch.

Okay. What do you want to do?

Can I see the mice?

Let me put the dishes away and grab my hat. You
need a hat too. It's too bright out here without something on your head. Don't you have a cap?

I left it at home.

Then we better get you one.

They went out to the shed in the backyard and
Louis lifted the lid from the box and the mother ran

away, out over the side, and the pink babies crawled over one another and whimpered. The boy bent down closer and looked at them. Can I touch one?

Not yet, they're too little. In a week or so.

They watched the mice for a while. One of them crawled to the edge of the box and lifted its blind face.

What's he doing?

I don't know. Maybe he's smelling. He can't see anything yet. I better put the lid back over them.

Can I see them tomorrow?

Yes, but I don't want you to come in here without me.

They worked in the garden again, pulling weeds and watering the beets and under the tomatoes. At noon they went to Addie's house and ate lunch. When the boy went upstairs to play with his phone Addie said, I think you could come over tonight.

It's not too soon?

No, he likes you.

He doesn't say much.

But you can see how he studies you. He wants your approval.

I just think it's pretty tough right now for him.

It is. But you're helping. I appreciate that.

I'm enjoying it.

So will you come tonight?

We'll try it.

So at dark Louis walked over and she met him at the door. He's upstairs, she said. I told him you would be here.

How'd he take that?

He wanted to know how soon. And he wanted to know why you were coming.

Louis laughed. I'd like to have heard that. What'd you say?

I said you are a good friend and sometimes we get together at night and lie down and talk.

Well, that's not a lie, Louis said.

In the kitchen Louis drank his bottle of beer, Addie her glass of wine, then they both went upstairs to the boy's room. He was playing with the phone and Addie put it on the dresser and read to him while Louis sat in the chair. Later they went out leaving the light on and the door open and moved to her room. Louis changed clothes in the bathroom and came to bed. They talked for a while and held hands and fell asleep. In the night the boy's screaming woke them up and they hurried into his room. He was sweaty and crying, his eyes frantic.

What's wrong, honey? Did you have a bad dream?

He kept crying and Louis picked him up and carried him back to the other room and settled him in the middle of the big bed.

It's all right, son, Louis said. We're both here. You can sleep with us for a while. We'll be on each side of you. He looked at Addie. We'll be a little group, with you in the middle.

He got into bed. Addie went out of the room.

Where's Grandma going?

She's coming back. She just has to use the bathroom.

Addie returned and lay down on the other side. I want to turn the light off now, she said. But we're all here.

Louis took the boy's hand and held it and the three of them lay together in the dark.

Good old dark, Louis said. All comfortable and good, nothing to worry anybody, nothing to be afraid of. He began to sing very softly. He had a good tenor voice. He sang "Someone's in the Kitchen with Dinah" and "Down in the Valley." The boy relaxed and went to sleep.

Addie said, I've never heard you sing before.

I used to sing to Holly.

You've never sung for me.

I didn't want to scare you away. Or have you send me away.

That was nice, she said. Sometimes you're a pretty nice man.

I suppose we're going to have to stay like this, divided all night.

I'll think good thoughts across to you.

Don't make them too racy. It might disturb my rest.

You never know.

19

There was one summer evening when Louis drove Addie and Jamie and Ruth out to Shattuck's Café on the highway for hamburgers. The old neighbor lady sat in front with Louis, Addie and the boy in back. The young girl took their orders and came back with their drinks and napkins and the hamburgers and they ate in the car. The highway was behind them and there wasn't much to look at, just the backyard of a small gray house across the lot. When they were finished Louis said, We better get some root beer floats to take with us.

Where are you taking us? Ruth said.

I thought we should watch some softball.

Oh, now I haven't done that for thirty years, she said.

It's time then, Louis said. He ordered four floats and he drove to the ballpark out behind the high school and stopped under the high bright field lights, parking with the car pointed toward home plate from the fence in the outfield.

I think Jamie and I'll go watch from the bleachers for a while.

Then I'll get up in front with Ruth, Addie said. We can visit and still see the game.

Louis and the boy took their floats and walked in front of the other cars and along the chain-link fence and climbed up into the wooden bleachers behind home plate. People said hello to Louis and asked who the boy was. This is Addie Moore's grandson, he told them. We're getting acquainted. They sat down behind some high school boys. The women were playing a team from the next town over and wore red T-shirts and white shorts. They looked pretty out under the bright lights on the green grass. Their arms and legs were all tanned. The local team was ahead by four runs. The boy didn't seem to know anything about the game so Louis explained as much as he thought he could take in.

Don't you ever play ball? Louis said.

No.

Do you have a glove?

I don't know.

Do you know what a softball glove is?

No.

You see what those girls have on their hands. That's a softball glove.

They watched for a while. The local women scored three more runs, people in the stands yelled and hollered, Louis yelled to one of the players and she looked up in the stands and saw him and waved.

Who's that?

One of the girls I used to teach. Dee Roberts, a smart girl.

Out in the car Addie and Ruth had rolled the windows down. Do you need to go to the grocery yet? Addie said.

No. I don't need anything.

You'll let me know.

I always do.

I'm afraid you don't.

I just don't eat much anymore. But I'm not hungry so it doesn't matter.

They watched the game and Addie honked the horn whenever the local team scored.

I know Louis still comes over, Ruth said. I see him going home in the mornings.

We decided it was all right even with Jamie here.

Yes. Children can accept and adjust to almost anything, if it's done right.

I don't think we're hurting him. We don't do anything, if that's what you mean.

No. I didn't mean that.

We don't anyway. We haven't.

You better get to going. You don't want to be as old as me.

Louis and Jamie climbed down and dumped the cups in the trash barrel and went back to the car. Addie got in the rear seat and they drove back to Cedar Street. Louis helped Ruth up to her front door and went home, and later he went over to Addie's house. Jamie was already asleep in the middle of her bed.

Thanks for this evening, Addie said.

Did you know he's never played catch before?

No. But his father was never much of an athlete.

I think every boy ought to have a chance to play catch.

I'm tired, she said. I'm getting into bed. You can talk to me about it there, in the dark. I'm worn out. All this excitement for one night.

20

The next day Louis took Jamie to the old Holt hardware store on Main Street and bought him a leather glove and one for himself and another for Addie and also three hard rubber balls and a small bat. At the counter he asked Jamie which of the caps on the display rack he wanted and the boy chose one in purple and black and the little stooped man at the register adjusted the back of the cap for him and the boy pulled it down and looked up at them with a serious look on his face.

Looks okay to me, Louis said.

That cap'll keep you from getting burned up out here in this sun, the little man said. Rudy was his name, Louis knew him from years ago. It was a wonder he was still working, a wonder that he was still alive. The other manager, a tall man named Bob, had died years ago. And the woman who owned the store had gone back to Denver after her mother died.

They returned to Louis's house and Louis showed him how to turn his glove in the right way to catch a ball and they played catch in the shade between Addie's house and Ruth's. The boy wasn't any good at first but got a little better after a while and then he wanted to try hitting with the bat. He finally hit one and Louis praised him extravagantly and they hit some more and then played catch again and the boy was improving now.

Addie came out from the house and watched. Can you stop now? I've got lunch ready. What have you got there? A baseball glove?

And I got this new cap.

I see you have. Did you thank Louis?

No.

You'd better, don't you think?

Thank you, Louis.

You're welcome.

We got a glove for you too, Jamie said.

Oh, I don't know how.

You have to learn, Grandma. I did.

That night in bed after Jamie was asleep between them Louis said, This boy needs a dog.

What makes you say that?

He needs someone or something to play with besides his phone and an old man and an old woman doddering around.

Thank you very much, Addie said.

But I'm serious, he does need a dog. What if we drive over to Phillips tomorrow and look at the humane shelter.

I don't want a puppy around here. I don't have the energy for a puppy.

No, a full-grown dog. One that's house-trained already. A nice small older dog.

I don't know. I don't know if I want the bother.

I'll keep it at my house. Jamie can come over and they can play there.

Do you want a dog around all the time? You surprise me.

I don't mind. It's been too long since I've had a dog.

I guess it's up to you. I wouldn't have thought of it myself.

After breakfast they drove out north of Holt on the narrow blacktop state highway past the fields of irrigated corn and the dryland wheat and turned west at Red Willow and went on past the country school in the next county and then north again down into the Platte

River valley and the town of Phillips. The humane shelter was on the edge of town. They told the woman at the front desk that they wanted a grown mature dog.

Well, we have more of that kind than anything else, she said. Did you have something specific in mind?

No. Just a dog that's not too wild or crazy or doesn't yap and bark all day long.

You want one for this boy to play with. Well, let's see what we've got.

She stood up heavily and led them back across the office. As soon as she opened the door the dogs in the cages and pens put up a frantic racket so that you could hardly hear what anyone said. They went in and she shut the door behind them. There were cages along either side of the middle walkway, with one or two dogs in each cage, with a bad smell in the room, cement floors in the cages and water bowls and pieces of carpet and rugs for the dogs to lie on.

I'll just let you look at the dogs yourselves. If you want to try one let me know.

Can we take any outside?

Yes, but you'll need a leash for that. Here's one hanging on the door here.

She left and they walked back past all the pens and looked in at each of them. There were all kinds and colors of dogs. The boy was afraid of the loud barking and kept close to Louis on the walkway. They turned and looked again at all the dogs.

Did you see any you liked?

I don't know.

What about this one? Addie said. It was a black and white border collie mix with something on its right front foot, a kind of bandage or plastic tube. She seems nice, Addie said.

What's on her foot? Jamie said.

I don't know. We can ask. It seems to be something to protect her.

Louis put his fingers through the mesh and the dog sniffed his fingers and licked at them. Let's take her outside. He opened the cage and went in and put the leash on her collar and blocked the other dog from coming out. He led her out easily, without trouble, and they went back into the office.

You found one, the woman said.

Maybe, Louis said. We want to take her outside to see how she is away from these other dogs.

You have to just stay here in the parking lot.

They went outside and across the lot past the parked cars and over to the weeds and dirt at the side. The dog immediately squatted. Good dog, Louis said. She waited until we got outside and over to the dirt. You want to lead her, Jamie?

Let's touch her first, Addie said.

They all bent down over her and she sat down on her haunches. The boy patted her head and she looked up at him.

You want to try now? I'll be right here with you.

Do you think she's all right? What about her foot?

We'll ask the woman inside. She limps a little when she walks but she doesn't seem to be in a lot of pain.

Jamie took the leash and the dog stood up and followed along beside him. Louis and the boy and the dog made a circle around the cars on the paved lot. Louis said, You want to try it by yourself? The boy and the dog took another little circle. They could see he liked her. They went back inside. She went in limping, favoring her right paw. The woman told them the dog had gotten her foot frozen in the winter when someone left her outside all night tied up on the back concrete patio. The veterinarian had had to amputate the toes on that foot. She had a white plastic tube she wore now that fastened with Velcro. If she was in the house they could take it off during the day and just have it put on only when she went out. The woman showed them how to take the tube off and how to put it on.

How old is she? Louis said.

About five, I'd guess.

I think we'll try her, Louis said. If it doesn't work out we can bring her back.

Well, we want people to make a good try, not to give up too soon.

We'll do that. But I want to know we can come back if we have to.

Yes, you can.

Louis paid the fee and collected her papers, the record of her inoculations, and they went out to the car. Jamie got in back and Louis put the dog in the seat beside him and they started out of town on the state highway toward home. After a while the dog laid her head on the boy's leg and shut her eyes and the boy patted her. Addie nodded for Louis to look in back, and he adjusted the mirror. They were both asleep now. In Holt, Louis dropped Addie off and at home he helped Jamie make a bed for the dog in the kitchen. You want to show her around the house? he said.

I've never been in the other rooms myself, Jamie told him.

That's right. He led the two of them through the house and at the stairs the dog loped up ahead of them, on three legs, holding her one paw up, and then they went back down to the kitchen. Let's see if your grandmother has any lunch for us.

What about our dog?

I think we'd better take her with us. She's just new. We don't want to leave her alone yet.

The boy took the leash and they went across the street and back through the alley to Addie's and knocked and went in.

In the kitchen Addie said, Have you decided on a name? She has to have a name. Didn't the woman call her something at the shelter?

Tippy, Louis said. But I don't like that very much.

What about Bonny? the boy said.

Where'd you get that name?

A girl in my class.

Someone you like?

Sort of.

All right. Bonny it is.

I think it suits her, Addie said.

Jamie and Louis left the dog on her rug at Louis's house out in the kitchen and went over to eat supper at Addie's. After supper they all went to check on her and she was whining and crying. They could hear her from a distance.

Why don't you just bring her over to my house for now? Addie said. I don't think Ruth and the other neighbors need this.

Then what?

Then we'll have to see.

They got the dog and brought her back to Addie's. Addie gave her an old throw rug to lie on and she settled down and watched them, looking one to the other. The boy went upstairs to play with his phone and took the dog with him. When Louis and Addie went up they told him the dog would have to stay in the kitchen. But after they took her downstairs, she began to cry again until Addie said, Oh, go ahead. I know what you want.

Louis said, Well, we don't want to hear that all night, do we?

I said go ahead.

He brought her to the front bedroom. Jamie looked over the side of the bed at her and reached down and petted her.

I've got another idea, Louis said. How about you and Bonny go into your bedroom? You can keep her with you.

I don't know.

She'll be right there with you in your room. You won't be alone.

When the boy got into bed the dog jumped up immediately.

Is this okay?

We'll try it. Unless your grandmother says not to.

But still leave the light on.

I will.

And the door open?

Now see if you can sleep. Bonny will be here with you.

Then Louis went back to the bed with Addie and slid in under the sheet.

Tell me something, she said.

What.

Did you have this in mind all along?

I wish I were that smart, Louis said. At least we can stretch out now without tangling up with a little boy's feet.

Addie turned off the light. Where's your hand?

Right here beside you where it always is.

She took his hand. Now we can talk again, she said.

What do you want to talk about?

I want to know what you're thinking.

About what?

About being over here. How it feels by now. Staying here at night.

I've gotten so I can stand it, he said. It feels normal now.

Just normal?

I'm trying to have some fun with you.

I know you are. Tell me the truth.

The truth is I like it. I like it a lot. I'd miss it if I didn't have it. What about you?

I love it, she said. It's better than I had hoped for. It's a kind of mystery. I like the friendship of it. I like the time together. Being here in the dark of night. The talking. Hearing you breathe next to me if I wake up.

I like all that too.

So talk to me, she said.

Is there anything specific?

Something more about yourself.

Aren't you tired of that?

Not yet. I'll tell you when I am.

Let me think a minute. You know that dog is on the bed with him.

I expected that.

She's going to get your bed dirty.

It'll wash. Now talk to me. Tell me something I haven't heard yet.

21

I wanted to be a poet. I don't think anyone but Diane ever knew that. I was studying literature in college and getting a teaching certificate at the same time. But I was crazy about poetry. All the standard poets that we read then. T. S. Eliot. Dylan Thomas. e.e. cummings. Robert Frost. Walt Whitman. Emily Dickinson. Individual poems by Housman and Matthew Arnold and John Donne. Shakespeare's sonnets. Browning. Tennyson. I memorized some of them.

Can you still recall them?

He said the opening lines of "The Love Song of J. Alfred Prufrock." A few lines of "Fern Hill" and some of the lines of "And Death Shall Have No Dominion."

What happened?

You mean why didn't I pursue it?

You still seem interested.

I am. But not like I was. I started teaching and

Holly came along and I got busy. I went to work in the summers painting houses. We needed the money. Or at least I thought we did.

I remember you painting houses. With a couple of other teachers.

Diane didn't want to work and I agreed it was important for Holly to have someone at home with her. So I wrote a little in the evening and a little maybe on the weekends. I got a couple of poems accepted by journals and quarterlies, but most of what I sent out got rejected, got returned without a note. If I ever got anything from an editor, some word or phrase, I took that as encouragement and practically lived on it for months. It's not surprising looking back on it. They were awful little things. Imitative. Unnecessarily complicated. I remember one poem had a line in it using the phrase iris blue, which is all right, but I divided the word up into the i of ris blue.

What does it mean?

Who knows. Or cares. I showed that particular poem, one of the early ones, to one of my professors at college and he looked at it and looked at me for a while and said, Well, that's interesting. Keep working. Oh, it was pitiful stuff really.

But you might have gotten better if you'd kept at it.

Maybe. But it didn't work out. I just didn't have it in me. And Diane didn't like it.

Why not?

I don't know. Maybe it was a threat to her of some kind. I think she was jealous of my feeling about it and about the time it took me away to myself, being isolated and private.

She didn't support your wanting to do this.

She didn't have anything she wanted to do herself. Except take care of Holly. And later she was confirmed in her feelings and thoughts by the group of women she met with, like I told you.

Well, I wish you'd take it up again.

I think it's past my time for that. I've got you now. I feel pretty passionate about us, you know. But what about you? You've never said what you wanted to do.

I wanted to be a teacher. I started a course in college in Lincoln but I got pregnant with Connie and quit school. Later on I took a short course in book-keeping so I could help Carl, and as I said I became his part-time receptionist and did the books. When Gene started school I took a clerk's job in the Holt town offices, as you know, and stayed there a long time. Too long.

Why didn't you ever go back to teaching?

I think I was never really deeply involved or committed to that. It was just what women did. Teaching or nursing. Not everybody finds out what they really want, like you did.

But I didn't do it either. I only played at it.

But you liked teaching literature in the high school.

I liked it all right. But it wasn't the same. I was only teaching poetry a few weeks a year and not writing it. The kids didn't really give a damn about it. A few of them did. But not most of them. They probably look back on those years and hours as old man Waters going off again. Talking shit about some guy a hundred years ago who wrote some lines about a dead young athlete being carried through town on a chair, which they couldn't relate to, or imagine such a thing being done to themselves. I made them memorize a poem. The boys chose the shortest poem possible. When they got up to recite they were petrified, just nervous as hell. I almost felt sorry for them.

Here's a kid that's spent his first fifteen years learning how to drive a tractor and drill wheat and grease a combine and now somebody arbitrarily makes him say a poem out loud in front of other boys and girls who've been raising wheat and driving tractors and feeding hogs and now to pass and get out of English class he's got to recite "Loveliest of trees, the cherry now" and actually say the word loveliest out loud.

She laughed. But that was good for them.

I thought so. I doubt they thought it was. I doubt they even do now, looking back on it, except to have a kind of communal pride in having taken old man Waters's course and gotten through it, thinking it was a kind of rite of passage.

You're too hard on yourself.

I did have one very bright country girl who memorized the Prufrock poem word perfectly. She didn't have to do that. It was on her own, her own volition and decision. I only asked them to memorize something short. I actually got tears in my eyes when she said all those lines so well. She seemed to have a pretty good idea what the poem meant too.

Outside the dark bedroom suddenly the wind came up and blew hard in the open window whipping the curtains back and forth. Then it started to rain.

I better close the window.

Not completely. Doesn't it smell lovely. The loveliest now.

Exactly.

He rose and pulled the window down, leaving it partially open, and got back in bed.

They lay next to each other and listened to the rain.

So life hasn't turned out right for either of us, not the way we expected, he said.

Except it feels good now, at this moment.

Better than I have reason to believe I deserve, he said.

Oh, you deserve to be happy. Don't you believe that?

I believe that's how it's turned out, for these last couple of months. For whatever reason.

You're still skeptical about how long this will last.

Everything changes. He got up again from bed.

Where are you going now?

I'm going to check on them. They might've gotten scared by the wind and rain.

You might scare them going in there.

I'll be quiet.

Come back then.

The boy was asleep. The dog lifted her head from the pillow, looked up at Louis and lay back again.

In Addie's bedroom Louis put his hand out the window and caught the rain dripping off the eaves and came to bed and touched his wet hand on Addie's soft cheek.

22

The next time they checked in the shed behind Louis's house the mice had grown and now had dark hair and their eyes were open. They skittered around when Louis raised the lid. The mother wasn't there. They watched the little bright black-eyed mice crawl over one another and sniffle and hide. They're about ready to leave the nest, Louis said.

What will they do?

They'll do what their mother shows them. They'll go out and look for food and make nests themselves and connect up with some other mice and have babies.

Won't we see them again?

Probably not. We might see them in the garden or out around the garage and beside the walls and the base of the shed. We'll have to watch.

Why did the mother run away? She left them alone.

She's afraid of us. She's more afraid of us than of leaving her children.

But we won't hurt them, will we?

No. I don't want mice in the house but I don't mind them out here. Unless they get under the hood of the car and chew through the wiring.

How can they do that?

Mice can get in almost anywhere.

23

Addie said, You don't need to do that.

Yes I do, Ruth said. I want to repay the favor. For taking me out.

What can I bring, then?

Just bring yourself. And Louis and Jamie.

In the afternoon they went to the back door of Ruth's old house and she came out across the porch in her slippers and house dress and apron, her face and thin cheeks red from cooking. She let them in. Bonny was whining at the bottom of the steps. Oh, let her come in too. She won't be any trouble. The dog came scrambling up into the house. They followed and went into the kitchen, where the table was already set. It was very warm because of the oven. I was going to have us eat in here. But it's too hot now.

Louis stood in the doorway. You want to move to the dining room?

That's so much bother.

We'll just move everything in there. What if I open some of these windows.

Well, I doubt they'll even open. You can try.

He pried at the bay windows with a screwdriver and got two to open.

Oh. You did it. Well, men are good for some things. I'll say that much.

Damn right, Louis said.

They ate a supper of macaroni and cheese casserole and iceberg lettuce with Thousand Island dressing and canned green beans and bread and butter and iced tea poured from an old heavy glass pitcher and there was Neapolitan ice cream for dessert. The dog lay at Jamie's feet.

After supper Ruth took Jamie into the living room and showed him the pictures on the walls and on the bureau while Addie and Louis cleared the dishes and washed up.

Look here, she said. Where do you think this is?

I don't know.

This is Holt. This is how Holt looked back in the 1920s. Ninety years ago.

The boy looked up at her old thin wrinkled face and looked at the picture.

Oh, I wasn't alive then. I'm not that old. My mother told me about it. Trees on Main Street. All along the street. An old-fashioned-looking place, orderly and quiet. Wasn't it pretty. Nice to walk there and shop. Then they got electricity. And light poles and street lights on Main Street. Then one night they cut all the trees down after people in town had gone to bed. The next morning people saw what the town council had done. They said the trees blocked the light from the street lamps. People were mad as hell about it, mad enough to spit. My mother was still mad about it for years afterward. She's the one who told me about this piece of town history and kept this old picture. Men, she used to say. She never forgave my father. He was on the town council.

Wait now, Louis said. I thought you said we were good for some things.

No. You're still on probation. But this boy can be different, she said. I have hopes for him. She took Jamie's face in her hands. You're a good boy. Don't you forget that. Don't you let anyone make you think otherwise. You won't, will you.

No.

That's right. She let him go.

Thank you for supper, he said.

Well, honey, you're very welcome.

They started home then. Addie, Louis, Jamie and the dog went out into the cool summer dark. It's a beautiful night, Addie called.

Yes, Ruth called. Yes. Goodnight.

24

One morning while it was still cool they took Bonny out in the country to let her run. They put the protective tube on her foot and drove out to the west of town onto a straight gravel road. There were sunflowers in the barrow ditch and short bluestem and soapweed. Jamie let the dog out of the back seat and took the leash off. She looked up at him, waiting.

Go on, Louis said. You can run now. Take off. He clapped his hands.

She jumped up and began running down the road and in and out of the barrow ditches, her protected paw making a soft thud in the hard road as she ran. The boy ran out after her. Addie and Louis followed, walking slowly, watching them. No cars came on the road while they were there.

This has been a good idea, Addie said, getting this dog.

He does seem happier.

That and he's made an adjustment to being here with us. Who knows if it'll continue when he goes home.

They came running back. The boy was red-faced and panting.

She can run all right with her hurt paw, he said. Did you see her?

The dog looked at the boy and they ran off again. It was getting hot now. Middle of July. The sky unclouded and the wheat in the fields alongside the road already cut, the stubble all neat and sheared off square, in the next field the corn running in straight dark green rows. A bright hot summer's day.

25

In late July Ruth went to the bank on Main Street with another old lady who was still permitted to drive, and standing at the teller counter she took up the money she was withdrawing from savings, folded it into her purse and zipped the pocket and turned to leave, and turned halfway around toward the door and fell down and died. Just collapsed in a final frail bundle on the tiled bank floor and stopped breathing. They said afterward that she had probably stopped breathing before she even hit the floor. The other woman covered her mouth with her hand and began to cry. They called for the ambulance but she was long past saving. They didn't bother taking her to the hospital. The coroner came to certify her death and they took her to the funeral home in town on Birch Street. Her body was cremated and there was a small funeral at the Presbyterian church two days later. Not many of her friends were still alive, old ladies, a few old men, who came limping and shuffling into the church and sat down in the pews and some of them leaned and nodded over with their chins rested on their thin chests and slept a while and then woke when the hymn started.

Addie and Louis sat down in front. She had arranged the funeral and told the minister about Ruth. He hadn't known her at all. She had stopped going to any church because of her feelings about orthodoxy and the childish ways in which churches talked and thought about God.

Afterward the people attending the funeral all went back to their silent homes and Addie took the enameled urn of her ashes to her house. It turned out the old lady had no immediate family, except for a distant niece in South Dakota who became her inheritor. The niece came to Holt in the next week and met with the lawyer and the realtor, and the house that Ruth had lived in for decades was sold in a month to a retired man and his wife from out of state. The niece didn't want the urn. Do you want it? she said.

Addie took it and at two in the morning in the dark she and Louis spread her ashes in the backyard behind Ruth's house.

Now it wasn't the same as it was when Ruth was there and they could all go out for a night to the drive-in café and afterward to a softball game. They decided Jamie didn't have to know about all of this. They told him she had gone to live somewhere else. They decided that wasn't entirely a lie.

She was a good person, wasn't she, Louis said. I admired her.

I miss her already, Addie said. What's going to happen to us—to you and me?

26

Addie said, After Connie's death Carl wasn't himself. He seemed all right on the outside when he was with other people away from home and at his office, but it changed him. He loved our daughter. More than me. More than Gene. He didn't pay as much attention to Gene after that and when he did it was often critical, to correct him. Many times I talked to him about it and he said he would try to do better. But it was never the same and it affected Gene. I know it did. I tried to make up for that but that didn't work either.

What about you and him? That must have changed too.

We stopped making love for a year after Connie's death. He wasn't interested. Then when he was interested again it wasn't much good. It was more just physical than anything loving and emotional. After a year or so we stopped altogether.

When was that?

Ten years before he died.

Did you miss it?

Of course. I missed the closeness more. We weren't at all close anymore. We were cordial and sort of formally pleasant and polite, but that was all.

I didn't know any of this. I didn't notice.

No, but how would you have noticed? In public we were kind, even affectionate. And we didn't see you very much even if we were neighbors. But nobody knew really. I didn't tell anyone and I'm sure Carl didn't. Gene knew but he may have come to think that that's the way it goes, how life is. That married people were that way to each other.

That seems pretty miserable to me.

Oh, it was bad. I tried talking but he wouldn't talk. I tried coming to bed naked. Put on perfume. I even ordered skimpy little nightgowns from a catalog. He thought it was disgusting. He got rough, kind of mean, when we did make love, the few times we did. Of course it wasn't love at all. He made me feel worse. I quit trying to fix things and we settled into our long polite and quiet life. I took Gene to Denver to concerts and plays and tried to give him more than just this house and its secrets, to get him out of Holt, and show him a larger world. I can't say that worked well either. Gene stayed closed up like his father. He got more so in high school, then he went off to college and we didn't see him even as much as we did before. So I began to go to Denver myself to plays and concerts. I treated myself. I felt I deserved it. I stayed at the Brown Palace Hotel and went out alone for expensive dinners. I bought a few dresses that I wore only in Denver. I didn't want to show myself in Holt in those clothes. I didn't want people to know. I expect people knew something anyway. Your wife may have.

If she did she never said anything about it to me.

I always liked that about Diane. I thought she was someone you could trust not to gossip or talk meanly.

But you still slept together all those years. You didn't want separate beds.

I suppose that sounds strange. But somehow that was what little we kept. We never touched each other. You learn how to stay strictly on your side and not to touch even by accident in the night. You take care of each other when you're sick and in the daytime you each do what you think of as your job. Carl would bring me flowers to make up and people in town would think, How nice. But all the time there'd be this secret of silence.

Then he died, Louis said.

Yes. I took care of him all along. I wanted to do that.

I needed to. He was sick off and on before he died that Sunday morning in the church. So yes, I took care of him. I don't know what else I would have done. We had that long time of joined life, even if it wasn't good for either one of us. That was our history.

27

At midweek they packed Louis's pickup and drove west up out of the plains toward the mountains, watching the mountains rise up higher as they got closer to the Front Range, the dark forested lower foothills and farther back the white peaks above tree line still with patches of snow even in July, and drove onto U.S. Highway 50 and went on through the few towns. They stopped in one of the towns for hamburgers and then drove up the highway through the Arkansas River canyon, the beautiful fast water, steep red jagged cliffs on each side, there were Rocky Mountain sheep along the road, all ewes with short sharp horns, and went on and then turned off toward North Fork Campground on County Road 240 and entered the national forest. There were not many people or campers in the campground. They got out and began to unload the pickup at a site near the creek. They could hear it running and rushing. The clear icy water, with brook trout holed up in the hollows below the rocks. There were tall fir trees and big ponderosas and aspen along the creek and back in the hillside. Tent and camper sites were marked off by timbers and there were picnic tables and firepit rings nearby.

We'll look around after we get camp set up, Louis said.

The boy helped set up the tent where Louis said was a good flat smooth place that wasn't too close to the fire ring. Louis showed him how to position the tent poles and stretch the guide ropes tight and peg them in the ground and how to fold back the window coverings and the door flap. They put their blowup mattresses and sleeping bags inside, Jamie and Bonny to sleep on one side, Addie and Louis on the other. Addie unzipped one of the bags and spread it out for herself and Louis and unzipped the other and laid it over the first sleeping bag, so they could have a wide comfortable bed together, and spread out another bag for Jamie.

Then the camp was set up and they went over to the creek and waded in the icy waters.

It's too cold, Grandma.

It comes straight out of a snowbank, honey.

By now it was getting dark, long past suppertime. Louis and the boy hauled wood from the pickup since cutting any limbs or trees wasn't permitted in the national forest. Jamie gathered up twigs and little dry branches from the ground and they laid a small fire inside the circle of rocks and propped a grate over it and Addie and the boy cooked hot dogs and canned beans in an iron frying pan and got out some raw carrots and chips. When the food was hot they sat down at the picnic table and ate and watched the fire.

You want to get some more wood? Louis said.

Jamie and the dog went out of the firelight to the pickup and the boy brought an armload of wood back.

Go ahead and lay some of it on, Louis said.

He put a piece of the wood on the fire, his arm stretched out, his eyes watering and blinking in the smoke. Then he sat down again. The air was cool and fresh, a mountain breeze blowing up. They didn't talk but looked at the fire and at the stars just above the mountains. They could see the bare peak of Mount Shavano shining in the night sky to the north.

Then Louis took Jamie down along the creek and cut three green willow shoots and sharpened the ends and went back to the campfire. Your grandma has a surprise for you.

What is it?

Addie got out a bag of marshmallows and poked one over the sharp end of each of the sticks.

Hold it near the fire. Let it brown up and get soft.

He held it out and it flamed up at once.

Blow on it.

Addie showed him how to brown it slowly by turning the stick. They ate two or three each. Jamie's mouth and hands got sticky with the sweet insides and blackened with marshmallow ash.

When they finished eating they put the food in the pickup cab for the night so it wouldn't attract bears. Then Louis took Jamie to the campground toilet and went in with him with a flashlight.

Just do your business and come out, Louis said. We don't have to linger in here. You want me to stay with you?

It stinks in here.

Louis pointed the flashlight down into the gaping dark hole of the tank.

Go ahead. I'm not leaving you.

Louis turned away and the boy pulled down his pants and sat on the seat with the open tank under him. He was afraid of it. When he was done Louis used the toilet and they went outside where the dog was waiting. They breathed again in the fresh air. They walked over and washed their hands and faces at the pump and went back to the tent.

It stinked in there, Grandma.

I know.

She got Jamie ready for bed in the sleeping bag with Bonny lying on the pillow beside him.

Where will you be?

We'll be sleeping here, right next to you.

All night?

Yes.

He went to sleep and Louis and Addie came into the tent after an hour and got undressed and lay down and held hands and looked at the stars up through the mesh window of the tent. There was the sharp pine smell of the trees.

Isn't it nice like this, Addie said.

In the morning they had pancakes and eggs and bacon and then tidied up the camp and put the food and cooking pans in the cooler in the back of the pickup and drove up farther in the mountains on the highway to Monarch Pass and stopped and got out at the Continental Divide and looked out over the western slope and if their eyes had been good enough and if they could have seen over the curvature of the earth they could have seen the Pacific Ocean a thousand miles away across the mountains. At noon they drove back to their camp and ate cheese sandwiches and apples and drank cold water from the old-fashioned well, pumping it out with the green pump handle, and then took a hike up to the waterfalls on North Fork Creek and sat and watched the water crash down into the clear green pool below. When they hiked down to the bottom, the air was cooler near the falls, the air misted on their faces.

They returned to camp and Addie and Louis set up folding camp chairs in the shade by the creek and read their books. The boy and the dog wandered around in the surrounding trees.

Can we take a walk somewhere, Jamie said.

You can follow the creek, Louis said. Which way do you think it's running?

Down there.

Why is that?

I don't know.

Because it's going downhill. Water always wants to flow to a lower place. Where do you want to go?

That way.

That's downhill. Down-river. To get back here to camp what would you do?

Turn around.

Smart boy. Follow the creek up-river and come back to our tent. Your grandma and I'll be waiting for you. Try it once. Go a little ways and then come back. Take Bonny with you. But don't cross the creek anywhere. Stay on this side.

The boy and the dog went down away from the campground and came back and then went farther down and poked around in the rocks and examined the shining mica and climbed on the big boulders and lay looking down into the water. Then they moved back up the creek.

What did you see? Louis said.

We didn't see any bears. But there was a deer.

What did Bonny do?

She barked at it. We just turned around. That's all we did.

In the evening they made another small fire and Addie cut up onions and peppers and put them in butter in the iron skillet and put in the ground-up hamburger and tomato sauce and a spoonful of sugar and Worcestershire sauce and a quarter cup of ketchup and salt and pepper, a sauce she'd made before they left home, and now stirred it all together and laid a lid on the pan. Louis and Jamie got out the hamburger buns and the leftover chips from the day before and set everything ready on the table, all the plates and unbreakable cups. Jamie took the dog and the empty jug down to the pump and came back with sweet fresh water, and the three of them ate sitting by the fire as the night came down. The boy gave Bonny some of his sloppy joe and looked at Louis to see what he thought. Louis winked and looked off into the trees.

Will we see any bears tonight? Jamie said.

I doubt it, Louis said. If we do it'll be a black bear. But they won't hurt us unless they get scared. Bonny would warn us anyway.

I'd like to see one from the pickup. From inside.

That'd be the way all right.

Are you worried about it? Addie said.

I just would like to see one.

They poured water on the fire, and the wood steamed and smoked, and the red coals blinked out, and then Louis took Jamie out into the trees with the flashlight shining ahead. He stopped.

You can pee here, he said. We don't have to go to the toilet when it's dark like this.

I'm not supposed to do it outside.

It's all right this time. Nobody will see us. He turned the light off. The animals pee out here. I guess we can this once.

They both peed on the ground and afterward Louis turned the flashlight on and let Jamie carry it. The light flickered and looped up and down on the trees and underbrush. They walked back to the tent.

The next day they drove down out of the mountains

back onto the plains. Other people were coming up now for the weekend towing big campers that looked out of place in the forest.

When they got down on the plains the air was hot and dry and the country seemed flatter than it had been and more bare and treeless. They reached home after dark and were tired, they showered and went to bed right away in their two separate rooms.

28

In early August Gene came out from Grand Junction to visit and Addie and Jamie met him at the door.

I don't see the dog you've been telling me about, he said.

She's at Louis's house, Jamie said.

You call him Louis?

Yes. He said to.

They went in and Gene took his bags upstairs to the back bedroom where Jamie and the dog slept and put the bags on the bed.

I'll stay in here with you in my old room.

What about Bonny?

She can't sleep in here with both of us.

She always sleeps with me.

We'll see how it goes.

They went back downstairs and in the late afternoon Louis came over to say hello and he brought the dog along. Jamie knelt down in front of her and petted her and took her outside to play in the yard.

Stay out of the street, Gene said.

We do this all the time, Dad. They went on out.

Gene looked at Louis. I hear you stay here with my mother too.

Some nights I do.

What's that about?

Friendship. For one thing.

What are you doing? Addie said. You know about this.

What am I doing? My mother's sleeping with an old neighbor man while my son's in the other room and I'm not supposed to ask about it.

That's right. How can this be any of your business?

It's my business if my son is here.

There's nothing to see, Louis said. I don't think it's hurting him. I wouldn't be here if I thought so.

I don't think you're the one to judge. You're getting what you want. Why would you care about a boy that belongs to somebody else?

But I do care about him.

Well, you can stop. I don't want him to be affected by this. I know about you. When I was a kid I heard about you.

What about me?

How you left your wife and daughter for some other woman.

That was over forty years ago.

It still happened.

And I'm sorry it did. But I can't go back and fix it now. Louis watched him for a moment. I think I'll leave. This isn't helping anything.

I'll call you later, Addie told him.

He stood and went out.

Why are you being this way? Addie said. What's wrong with you?

I don't want my son to be hurt.

You don't think he's already been hurt by his father and mother this summer?

Yes, I do think so. And now it's getting worse.

You don't know what you're talking about. He's far better now than when you left him here. And if you want to know the truth Louis has been good for him.

Because he's after your money too, isn't he?

Whatever are you talking about now?

If you married him he'd get half of everything, wouldn't he? I couldn't stop him.

We're not getting married. And he's not interested in my money. My God, what little you must think of me.

He looked away. I don't know what I'm going to do. I've got to start over.

You know I'll help you.

For how long?

As long as it takes. As long as I can.

You're getting tired of it already. You must be.

Well, I'm still doing it. You're my son. Jamie's my grandson.

The next two nights the dog stayed with Louis at his house and the boy slept upstairs in the back room with his father and on the second night, Sunday night, he had a bad dream and woke up crying and would not be consoled until Addie came in and held him and took him back into her bed. On Monday Gene told them good-bye and drove home.

When his father was gone the boy went to Louis's house and put on the dog's leash and the protective tube on her paw and came out with her and walked around the block and up the alley to Addie's backyard and played with her there while she and Louis watched him.

It was bad last night, Addie said. It was like when he first got here. Having those bad dreams. He was upset again. Now Gene tells me Beverly is coming back home in a couple of weeks.

What's going to happen then?

I don't know. They're going to try again, I guess. She'll move back in. And Jamie will start school.

He could take the dog with him when he goes. If they'd agree.

I don't know if they would.

Why don't you ask. It'd make some difference anyway.

They looked out at Jamie and Bonny in the backyard.

Should I come over tonight? Louis said.

You'd better, you dirty old man.

He didn't say I was dirty.

But I know, she said.

29

Louis said, It was awful for her that last year. She was just always sick. They tried chemotherapy and radiation and that slowed it for a while but it was still there and it never was out of her system completely. She got worse and she didn't want to have any more treatments. She was just wasting away.

I remember, Addie said. I wanted to help.

I know. You and all the others brought food. I appreciated that. And the flowers.

But I never saw her in her bedroom.

No. She didn't want any company upstairs except Holly and me. She didn't want anybody to see her, how she looked then in the last months. And she didn't want to talk. She was afraid of death. Nothing I said made any difference.

Aren't you afraid of death?

Not like I was. I've come to believe in some kind of

afterlife. A return to our true selves, a spirit self. We're just in this physical body till we go back to spirit.

I don't know if I believe that, Addie said. Maybe you're right. I hope you are.

We'll see, won't we. But not yet.

No, not yet, Addie said. I do love this physical world. I love this physical life with you. And the air and the country. The backyard, the gravel in the back alley. The grass. The cool nights. Lying in bed talking with you in the dark.

I love all that too. But Diane was worn out. At the end she was too tired and too weary to pay attention to her fears anymore. She wanted out, relief. An end to her suffering. She suffered terribly in the last months. So much pain. Even with sedatives and morphine. And she was still scared most of the time, underneath. I'd come in, I'd check her in the night and she'd be awake staring at the dark through the window. Can I help you? I'd say. No. Do you want something? No. I just want it to be over. Holly would help bathe her and would try to get her to eat but she wasn't hungry. She wouldn't eat anything. I suppose in some way she knew she was starving herself. She was so frail and tiny at the end, her legs and arms like sticks. Her eyes looking too big in her head. It was awful to watch and more than awful for her, of course. I wanted to do something for her and there wasn't a thing more to be done than what we were already doing. The hospice nurse came every day and was very good and helped make it possible for her to die at home. She didn't want to go back to the hospital ever. So that's how it was. Finally she died. Holly and I were both in the room. She stared at us with those big dark staring eyes like she was saying Help me Help me Why won't you help me. Then she quit breathing and was gone.

People say the spirit stays around for a while floating over the body and maybe hers did. Holly said she had the sense of her mother being in the room and maybe I did too. I couldn't be sure. I felt something. Some kind of emanation. But it was very slight, maybe just a breath. I don't know. At least she's at peace now in some other place or higher realm. I think I believe that. I hope she is. She never really got what she wanted from me. She had a kind of idea, a notion of how life should be, how marriage should be, but that was never how it was with us. I failed her in that way. She should've had somebody else.

You're being too hard on yourself again, Addie said. Who does ever get what they want? It doesn't seem to happen to many of us if any at all. It's always two people bumping against each other blindly, acting out of old ideas and dreams and mistaken understandings.

Except I still say that this isn't true of you and me. Not right now, not today.

I feel that too. But you might get tired of me too and want out.

If that happens we can stop, she said. That's the understood agreement for us, isn't it. Even if we never actually said so.

Yes, when you get tired of this, you can say so.

And you too.

I don't think I'll get there. Diane never got to have what we do. Unless she had somebody I didn't know about. She didn't, though. She wouldn't think that way.

30

In August there was the annual Holt County Fair and rodeo and livestock judging at the fairgrounds on the north side of town. It started with a parade coming up from the south end of Main Street, coming up the street toward the railroad tracks and old depot. It was raining the day of the parade. Louis and Addie put on raincoats and cut a hole in the end of a black plastic trash bag to put over Jamie and the three of them walked over to Main Street and stood along the curb with the other people. There were crowds along both sides of the street despite the weather. The honor guard came first, carrying the limp wet flags and shouldering dripping rifles, then there were old tractors muttering up the street and old combines on flatbed trailers and antique hay rakes and mowers, and more tractors, puttering and popping, and the high school band, reduced in the summer to only fifteen members wearing white shirts and jeans all soaking now and sticking to their skin, then the convertible cars with the county notables inside but with the tops up because of the weather, and then the rodeo queen and her attendants on horses, the girls all good riders wearing ranch slickers, followed by more fancy cars with advertisements on the doors, and cars for the Lions Club and the Rotary and Kiwanis and the Shriners zigzagging around in the street, like fat show-off kids, in their hopped-up go-carts, and more horses and riders in yellow slickers and a pony cart, and toward the end of the parade there was a flatbed truck with a cardboard religious picture on it and a riser at the front, entered in the parade by one of the evangelical churches in town. On the riser there was a wooden cross and a young man standing in front of it with long hair and a dark beard, wearing a white tunic and because of the rain he was holding an umbrella over his head. When Louis saw him he laughed out loud. The people standing nearby turned and stared at him.

You're going to get yourself in trouble, Addie said. This is serious here.

I guess he can walk on water, but he can't keep it from falling on his head.

Hush, she said. Mind your manners.

Jamie looked up at them to see if they were really angry.

At the end of the parade the Holt street cleaner came sweeping up the street with its big rotating brushes.

In the afternoon the rain stopped and they drove out to the fairgrounds and parked and walked through the stock barns past the sleek horses and the groomed cattle with their puffed-up ratted tails, and looked at the great hogs lying on the straw on the cement flooring in the pens, lying there fat and panting and pink, batting their ears, and they walked past the goats and sheep all trimmed and shaved, and then out through the cages of rabbits and chickens and around to the carnival area. They put Jamie on the Ferris wheel with Addie, Louis said the rides made him sick. Addie and the boy rode up and around and when they were at the top she pointed out Main Street and the grain elevator and water tower and pointed to where their houses were on Cedar Street.

Do you see my house?

No.

Right over there. With the big trees.

I don't see it.

They looked far out beyond the edge of town to the open country where they could see farmhouses and barns and the windbreaks. Afterward they tried some of the games, the rifle shoot and ball throw, and bought Jamie pink cotton candy on a paper cone, and icy slushy drinks for themselves and wandered around watching the people and then went back and she and the boy rode the Ferris wheel again. By now it was late afternoon. They could hear the rodeo still going on from the arena on the other side of the grandstands, the loud cheerful voice of the announcer. They didn't buy tickets to go into the rodeo stands but walked down past the far end and looked over the fence at the calf roping and bull riding. There was a quarter-mile horse race on the dirt track and they watched as the horses galloped by, the jockeys standing up now in their irons after they had passed the finish line, the horses wide-nostriled and stirred up. Then they went back to the car and drove home and the boy got the dog out of Louis's kitchen and they had supper on the front porch as the day was ending.

31

Louis mowed his lawn and then mowed Addie's and dumped the grass out of the rear catcher into a wheelbarrow and Jamie pushed it around back and tipped it out in the alley onto the musty pile there and came back for more. When they were finished Louis sprayed off the mower with the hose and put it away in the shed.

In the corner he lifted the lid from the nest box.

Do you think we'll ever see those mice again?

We might, Louis said. We'll have to keep watching.

I wonder where they went. I wonder if the mother ever found them.

They went into Addie's kitchen and drank iced tea and then went out into the side yard in the shade and played catch. Addie came out with them. Bonny raced back and forth chasing the ball and jumping in the air and grabbing it up when it hit the ground and ran in circles until they caught her.

At noon Louis went home and Jamie kept the dog with him at Addie's and ate lunch with her, talking quietly, and then he and Bonny went upstairs to the back bedroom and the dog lay sleeping at the foot of the bed in the warm room while he played with his phone and called his mother.

I'll be seeing you soon, his mother said. Didn't I tell you? I'm coming back home.

What does Dad say?

He says that's good. We both want to try again. Aren't you glad?

When will you come?

In a week or two.

Will you live in the house?

Of course. Where else would I live?

I don't know. Maybe some other place?

Honey, I want to be with you.

And Dad.

Yes, and Dad.

32

A few nights later Addie and Louis and Jamie went out to the Wagon Wheel restaurant on the highway east of town and sat at one of the tables near the big windows. There was a view of the wheatland out to the south. The sun was going down and the stubble was beautiful in the lowering light. After they ordered their dinner an old man walked over and sat down heavily in the vacant chair. A big solid-looking man in a long-sleeved shirt and new jeans, his face very red and wide.

Louis said, You know Addie Moore, don't you, Stanley?

Not as good as I'd like to.

Addie, this is the famous Stanley Thompkins.

I ain't too famous. More like infamous.

And this is Addie's grandson Jamie Moore.

Let me see your grip, son.

The boy reached out and shook the old man's thick hand and the old man winced and Jamie stared at him.

I heard you two was seeing each other, Stanley said.

Addie's willing to put up with me, Louis said.

Makes me think there might be hope for somebody else in this life.

Addie patted his hand. Thank you. It is a hopeful thing, isn't it.

You know anybody wants to curl up with a old wheat farmer?

I'll start looking, she said.

I'm in the phone book. I can be reached.

So what's happening? Louis said.

Oh, you know, the usual. My boy got the wheat in and took off for Vegas. He couldn't stand having a little money in the bank. Took some gal with him too from over at Brush. I never met her. I guess she's good looking.

Why didn't you go with them?

Oh hell. He looked at Jamie. Scuse me. I never got much out of sitting around with strangers messing with cards. If you was to have a game of poker at your house or somebody else here did, that would be a different story. You'd know who you was playing with and it would be more fun. But I'm no good in cities anyway.

How did your wheat do?

Well, it was pretty good this year, Louis. I don't want to say this out loud. But this was one of the best years we've had in a long time. The rain came at the right time and there was a lot of it and we never got no hail on our place. Our neighbor to the south did. But we was just lucky all around.

The waitress brought the plates of food.

I'm keeping you from your supper. He stood up and reached out to shake the boy's hand again. Now take it easy on me. The boy tentatively took his hand and barely touched him. Okay, I'll be seeing you.

Take care.

Good to meet you, Mrs. Moore.

After they'd finished eating they rode out to the country and drove to the Thompkins place northeast of town and stopped and looked at the stubble fields in the starlight and they all looked thick and even.

He must have done pretty well, Louis said. I'm glad of it. He's had bad years too. Everybody has.

But not this year, Addie said.

No. Not this year.

33

He died during church on a Sunday morning, Addie said. You know that.

Yes, I remember.

It was in August, it was hot in the sanctuary and Carl always wore a suit even in summer even on the hottest days. He thought it was what he had to do as a businessman, as an insurance agent. He had some notion about keeping up appearances. I don't know why or for whom it mattered. But it mattered to him. Halfway into the preacher's sermon I felt him leaning against me and I thought, He's gone to sleep. Well, let him sleep. He's tired. But then he slumped forward and bumped his head hard on the back of the pew in front of us before I could catch him. I reached for him but he just kind of folded forward out of the pew and dropped onto the floor. I bent over, I whispered to him, Carl. Carl. The people around us were watching him and the man sitting next to him slid over in the pew to try to help me lift him up. The preacher stopped talking and other people got up and came to try to help. Call the ambulance, someone said. We got him lifted off the floor and laid him out on the pew. I tried breathing into his mouth and pumping his chest but he was already gone. The ambulance men came. Do you want to take him to the hospital? they said. I said, No, take him to the funeral home. The coroner will have to come before we can move him, they said. So we waited for the coroner and then finally he came and pronounced Carl dead.

The ambulance took him over to the funeral home and Gene and I followed them in the car. The funeral director left us with him in the back room where it was sort of formal and quiet, not the room where they do the embalming. I said I didn't want him embalmed. Gene didn't want him embalmed either. He was home from college for the summer. So we sat in the room with his father's body. Gene wouldn't touch him. I bent over his face and kissed him. He was already cold by then and his eyes wouldn't stay shut. It was eerie and strange and very still in the room. Gene never did touch him. He went out of the room and I stayed there for a couple of hours and pulled a chair up beside him and leaned over and held his hand and thought of all the times that had seemed good between us. And eventually I told him good-bye and got the director and told him we were finished for now and that we wanted his body cremated and made the arrangements. It was all too sudden. I was in some kind of trance. I think I was just in shock.

You would be. Of course, Louis said.

But even now I can see it all clearly and feel that kind of otherworldliness, the sense of moving in a dream and making decisions that you didn't know you had to make, or if you were sure of what you were saying.

Gene was terribly upset by it. He wouldn't talk about it though. He was like his father in that. Neither one of them ever talked about things. Gene stayed here for a week then went back to college and was allowed into his apartment early and he stayed there the rest of the summer. It would have been better if we could have helped each other but that didn't happen. I don't think I tried too hard myself. I wanted him to stay but I could see it wasn't helping either one of us. We were just avoiding each other and when I tried to talk to him about his father he said, Nevermind, Mom. It doesn't matter now. Of course it did matter. He had a great buildup of anger and resentment toward Carl and

I don't think he's gotten free of it to this day. It's partly what affects his connection with Jamie. He seems to be repeating what happened between him and his own father.

You can't fix things, can you, Louis said.

We always want to. But we can't.

34

On a Sunday they sat at the kitchen table over their morning coffee. There was an advertisement in the *Post* about the coming theatrical season at the Denver Center for the Performing Arts. Addie said, Did you see they're going to do that last book about Holt County? The one with the old man dying and the preacher.

They did those other two so I guess they might as well do this one too, Louis said.

Did you see those earlier ones?

I saw them. But I can't imagine two old ranchers taking in a pregnant girl.

It might happen, she said. People can do the unexpected.

I don't know, Louis said. But it's his imagination. He took the physical details from Holt, the place names of the streets and what the country looks like and the location of things, but it's not this town. And it's not anybody in this town. All that's made up. Did you know any old brothers like that? Did that happen here?

Not that I know of. Or ever heard of.

It's all imagined, he said.

He could write a book about us. How would you like that?

I don't want to be in any book, Louis said.

But we're no more improbable than the story of the two old cattle ranchers.

But this is different.

How different? Addie said.

Well, it's us. We don't seem improbable to me.

You thought so at first.

I didn't know what to think. You surprised me.

Don't you feel okay now?

It was a good surprise. I'm not saying it wasn't. But I still don't understand how you got the idea of asking me.

I told you. Loneliness. Wanting to talk in the night.

It seems brave. You were taking a risk.

Yes. But if it didn't work I'd be no worse off. Except for the humiliation of being turned down. But I didn't think you would tell anyone about it so it would be just you and me who would know if you did turn me down. But everyone knows now. They have for months. We're old news.

We're not even old news. We're not even news of any kind at all, Louis said.

Do you want to be news?

No. Hell. I just want to live simply and pay attention to what's happening each day. And come sleep with you at night.

Well, that's what we're doing. Who would have thought at this time in our lives that we'd still have something like this. That it turns out we're not finished with changes and excitements. And not all dried up in body and spirit.

And we're not even doing what people think we're doing.

Do you want to? Addie said.

That's entirely up to you.

35

Toward the end of August Gene drove over the mountains and out to Holt on a Saturday to take his son home. He arrived at his mother's house late in the afternoon and came up and hugged them both and then walked down the street with Jamie and the dog.

Don't you like her?

Of course I do.

You don't ever touch her. You haven't petted her once.

He leaned down over the dog and patted her head and talked kindly to her and they went on around the block then back up to Addie's house through the alley. They ate supper and at night Gene slept with Jamie and the dog together in the same double bed in the back bedroom. Louis stayed away.

In the morning they packed up Jamie's clothes, toys and baseball stuff and the dog dish and food. Then the boy said, I have to say good-bye to Louis.

We need to go.

Just for a minute, Dad. I have to.

Don't take too long then.

He ran over to Louis's house but he wasn't home. He opened the door and called inside and ran through the rooms. He came back crying.

You can call him later, his father said.

It's not the same.

We can't wait. It's going to be late already by the time we get home.

Addie hugged him hard and said, Now you call me, you hear? I want to know how you're doing and how school is. Jamie was clinging to her. She gradually loosened his hands. Just be sure you call me.

I'll call, Grandma.

She kissed Gene. And you be patient.

I know, Mom.

I hope so. You call me too.

They started up, the boy and the dog together at the window in the back seat looking at her standing on the curb. The boy was still crying. Addie watched the car until it turned out of sight. By the time it was dark Louis had not come over to her house yet so she called him. Where are you? Aren't you coming over?

I didn't know if I should.

You don't understand yet, do you. I don't want to

be alone and brood like you do working things out by myself. I want you to come over so I can talk to you.

Let me clean up first.

You don't need to clean up.

Yes, I want to. I'll be there in an hour.

Well, I'll still be here, she said. I'll be waiting.

He shaved and showered as he always did and in the darkness of evening walked over past the neighbors' houses and she was sitting on the porch waiting for him and she got up and stood on the steps and kissed him for the first time where people could see them. You're so wrongheaded sometimes, she said. I don't know if you'll ever learn.

I never thought of myself as a slow learner. But I must be.

You are when it comes to me.

I know what I think of you and how much you mean to me. But I can't get it in my head that I mean anything like the same to you.

I'm not going into that again. That's your problem, not mine. Now let's go upstairs.

In bed they held each other in the dark and she said, I don't know how it's going to work out.

Are you still talking about us?

I'm talking about my son and grandson and the

boy's mother. He was crying when he left. Do you know why?

Because he's going to miss you.

Yes, she said. But he was crying because he didn't get to say good-bye to you. Where were you?

I went out to drive around in the country and then I decided to drive over to Phillips to eat lunch and didn't get back till late afternoon.

He went to your house to see you before he left. That's how much he cares for you.

I care about him too.

I just hope Gene and his wife can do better. Maybe they've learned something over the summer. I'm already worried about them.

What did you tell me? Something about not being able to fix people's lives.

That was for you, she said. Not for me.

I see, Louis said.

Oh I feel better already talking with you here next to me.

We haven't even said much of anything yet.

But I do feel better already. I thank you for that. I'm grateful for all of this. I feel very fortunate again now.

36

After Jamie had left they tried to do what the town thought all along they'd been doing but hadn't. By now Louis had long begun undressing in the bedroom, he got into his pajamas and was faced away from the bed where Addie was lying under a cotton sheet, and then he turned toward her and without his knowing she had drawn the sheet back and was lying naked on the bed in the low light of the bedside lamp. He stood looking at her.

Don't stand there, she said. You make me nervous.

Don't be, he said. You look lovely.

I'm too heavy around the hips and stomach. This old body. I'm an old woman now.

Well, old woman Moore. You've won me completely. You're just right. You're how you're supposed to look. You're not supposed to be some thirteen-year-old girl without any breasts and hips.

Well, I'm not that now if I ever was.

Look how I've turned out, he said. I've got this gut on me. My arms and legs are thin old man's arms and legs.

You look good to me, she said. But you keep standing there. Aren't you going to lie down? Are you just going to stand there all night?

Louis got out of his pajamas and slid into bed and she moved over closer to him and took his hand and kissed him and he turned on his side and kissed her and touched her shoulder and touched her breasts.

It's been a long time since anyone did that, she said.

It's been a long time since I've done anything like this.

He kissed her again and touched her and then she pulled him closer and he lifted in the bed and lay kissing her face and neck and shoulders and moved over and started to move and then stopped after a short while.

What's wrong?

I can't stay hard. I've got the old man's complaint.

Have you had this trouble before?

No. But I haven't tried this for years either. The limp time has come, as the poet says. I'm just an old son of a bitch now.

He lay back and settled beside her in the dark.

Do you feel bad? she said.

Yeah, a little. But more than anything I feel I've disappointed you.

You haven't. It's just the first time. We have all the time ahead of us.

Maybe I ought to try some of those pills they advertise on TV.

Oh, I think it'll be all right. Let's try again another night.

37

After dark one night they walked over to the grade school playground and Louis pushed Addie on the big chain swing and she rode up and back in the cool fresh night air of late summer with the hem of her skirt fluttering over her knees. Afterward they went back to bed in her upstairs front room and lay beside each other naked in the summer air coming in from the open windows.

And once they stayed overnight in Denver as she had before at the great old beautiful Brown Palace Hotel with its open court and lobby and the piano player who played all afternoon and evening. Their room was on the third floor and they could look over the railing down to the open courtyard below and see the piano player and people sitting at tables taking tea and drinking cocktails and the waiters moving back and forth from the bar and as night approached the guests going into the bar or into the restaurant with its white table-cloths and gleaming glasses and silverware. They went down and ate in the restaurant and then came back upstairs and Addie put on one of the expensive dresses she'd bought years ago just to wear in Denver. Then they went out onto the sidewalk to the 16th Street Mall and rode the shuttle bus to Curtis Street and walked over to the Denver Center and through the lobby and off to the left to the theater. A woman showed them to their seats, the theater a great large auditorium, and they looked all about at the other people coming in and talking and then the play began, the men on stage singing on their mission in their black pants and ties and white shirts, the audience amused by some of it. They held hands and at intermission went out to the restrooms. The women queued up in a long line. Louis went back to their seats and Addie returned just in time for the second half of the play.

Don't say anything, she said.

I'm not.

Why can't they figure it out that women take more time and need more stalls?

You know why, he said.

Because men are the ones who design these things, that's why.

They watched the second half and then went out

onto the street in the bright lights in front of the theater and caught a cab and rode back to the hotel.

Do you want a drink? he said.

Just one.

They walked into the bar and were shown to a table and each had a glass of wine, then they took the elevator to their room and undressed and got into the big king-sized bed. They shut the lights off and had just the light coming in from the street through the lacey curtain.

Isn't this fun, she said.

Sure seems so to me.

She scooted over close to him.

I'm about as happy as I can be, she said. This is just what I want and tomorrow I want our own bed again.

Everything in its time and place, he said.

Now are you going to kiss me in this big hotel bed or not?

I was hoping to.

In the morning they ate a late breakfast in the restaurant and then packed up and the valet brought Louis's car around to the front of the hotel and helped them with their bags. Louis gave him a generous tip out of his good feeling. They drove home leisurely on U.S. 34 out onto the high plains through Fort Morgan and Brush and finally into Holt County, all flat and treeless except in the windbreaks and along the streets in the little towns and around the farmhouses. There was a cloudless sky and nothing along the horizon but more blue sky.

They got to Addie's in the afternoon and Louis carried her bags up to her room and then took his car home and unpacked his bags. At dark he walked over to her house for the night.

38

Labor Day they decided to drive out east on the highway to Chief Creek. The creek was shallow and sandy-bottomed with grass and willows grown up on both sides and milkweed, the grass had been cropped off close to the ground by cattle. There were great old cottonwood trees in a grove back a little from the creek. Addie brought out the basket with their picnic and Louis got the rake and shovel from the car trunk and scraped the old dry flaky manure from the shade under the trees where the cattle had stood out of the wind.

You've been here before, Addie said. You came prepared.

We used to come out here when Holly was a little girl. It's about the only place to find running water and shade.

Well, it's nice. It's not the mountains but it's nice for Holt County.

Yes.

But won't somebody come to chase us off this place?

I doubt it. It belongs to Bill Martin. He never minded before.

You know him.

You do too, I think.

Just by name.

I had his kids in school. They were all bright kids. Hell-raisers, but bright. They've all left home now. I imagine he's sorry about that. Kids don't want to stay here.

Addie spread out a blanket on the cleared ground and they sat down and ate the fried chicken and cole-slaw and carrot sticks and chips and olives and she cut them each a piece of chocolate cake. They drank iced tea with it all. Then they lay down on the blanket and looked up into the green moving branches of the tree overhead, the leaves twisting and fluttering in the low wind.

After a while Louis sat up and took his shoes and socks off and rolled up his pants cuffs, then walked over to the creek across the hot ground and stepped down into the cool water onto the sandy bottom and dipped and cupped water onto his face and arms. Addie joined him, barefooted in her summer dress. She held her dress up above her knees and stepped in.

Oh isn't this just perfect for a hot day. I've never been here before. I didn't know there was anyplace like this in Holt County.

Stick with me, he said. You'll learn a lot, lady.

Louis took off his shirt and pants and underwear and laid them out on the grass and stepped back into the water, splashed himself and sat down.

Well then, Addie said. If that's the way you're going to be. She pulled her dress off over her head, took off her underwear and lowered herself into the cool water beside him. And I don't even care if someone sees us, she said.

They sat facing each other and lay back in the water, both of them very pale except for their faces and hands and arms. They were a little heavy, contented. They could feel the current pushing fingers of sand underneath them.

Later they got out and went back to the blanket and toweled off and got dressed, they took a nap in the warm afternoon in the shade of the trees and got up again and waded in the creek once more to cool off before they packed up the food and drove back to Holt. He dropped her off at her house and she carried the picnic basket inside while he drove down the block and parked his car and put the shovel and rake back in the shed. When he stepped into the house, the phone rang almost immediately.

You'd better come over here, Addie said.

What's going on?

Gene is here. He wants to talk to both of us.

I'll be there in a minute.

In the living room Gene was sitting on the couch across from Addie.

He said, Sit down, Louis.

Louis looked at him and walked across the room and kissed Addie on the mouth. He made a point of it. Then he sat down.

What's this about?

I'll get to that, Gene said. I've been waiting for you all afternoon.

I told him where we've been, Addie said.

It's not much of a place.

It's what you make of it. It's who you're with, Louis said.

That's why I'm here. I want this to stop.

You're talking about us being together, Louis said.

I'm talking about you sneaking over here at night to my mother's house.

No one's sneaking around, Addie said.

That's right. You're not even ashamed of yourselves.

There's nothing to be ashamed of.

People your age meeting in the dark like you do.

It's been lovely. I wish you and Beverly had as good a time together as Louis and I do.

What would Dad say if he was in my position?

He wouldn't want to talk about it. But I doubt he would have approved. It would not be something he would have done himself, even if he'd have thought of it.

No. He wouldn't have approved. He had more sense, a clearer idea of his standing.

Oh Jesus. I'm seventy years old. I don't care about what the town thinks. And you might care to know that at least some of the town does approve of us.

I don't believe that.

Well you can or not, it doesn't matter.

It matters to me. Taking my mother to Denver. Taking my son up in the mountains. And my God, the two of you sleeping in the same bed with him.

How do you know that? Addie said.

Nevermind. I know. What in the hell were you thinking of?

We were thinking about him, Louis said. He was scared. We brought him in to comfort him.

Yes, and every night now he cries. That started here.

That started, Addie said, when you left him here.

Mom, you know why I did that. You know I love my son.

But can't you just do that? Can't you just love him? He's a good little boy. That's all he wants.

Like Dad did with me, you mean.

I know your father wasn't always kind.

Kind. My God, he had nothing to do with me after Connie died.

Gene wiped at his eyes. He looked at Louis. I want you to stay away from my mother. To leave my son alone. And forget about my mother's money.

Gene, just be quiet, Addie said. Don't say any more. What's wrong with you?

Louis stood up from the couch. Listen to me, he said. It's too bad you feel like this. I would never hurt your son. Or your mother. But I won't stay away from her until she tells me to. And I sure as hell don't have any interest in her money. If you want to talk anymore about this to me, I'll see you tomorrow.

Louis bent over and kissed Addie again and went out.

I'm ashamed of you, Addie said. I don't know what to say to you. This whole thing makes me so sick. So sad.

Just stop seeing him.

In the night Addie pulled the covers up to her face and turned away from the window and wept.

39

After the talk with Gene, Addie and Louis still saw each other. He came to her house at night but it was different now. It was not the same lighthearted pleasure and discovery. And gradually there were nights when he stayed home, nights when she read for hours alone, not wanting him to be there in bed with her. She stopped waiting for him, naked. They still held each other in the night when he did come over but it was more out of habit and desolation and anticipated loneliness and disheartenment, as if they were trying to store up these moments together against what was coming. They lay awake side by side silently now and never made love anymore.

Then the day came when Addie tried to talk to her grandson on the phone. She could hear the boy crying in the background but his father wouldn't let him talk.

Why are you doing this? she said.

You know why. If I have to do this I will.

Oh you're just mean. This is cruel. I didn't think you'd go so far.

You can change it.

She called her grandson one afternoon when she thought he would be at home by himself. But he wouldn't talk to her.

They'll be mad, he said. He began to cry. They'll take Bonny away. They'll take my phone.

Oh God, Addie said. All right, honey.

When Louis came to her house in the middle of that week she led him out to the kitchen and gave him a beer and poured herself a glass of wine.

I want to talk. Out here in the light.

Something more has changed, he said.

I can't do this anymore, she said. I can't go on this way. I thought something like this was coming. I have to have contact, and some kind of life with my grandson. He's the only one left to me. My son and his wife mean little now. That's all broken, I don't think they or I will ever get over it. But I still want my grandson. This summer made that clear.

He loves you.

He does. He's the only one of my family who does. He'll outlive me. He'll be with me as I die. I don't want the others. I don't care about the others. They've killed that. I don't trust Gene. I can't guess what else he might do.

So you want me to go home.

Not tonight. One more night. Will you do that?

I thought you were the brave one of us.

I can't be brave anymore.

Maybe Jamie will fight it and call you on his own.

Not yet he won't. He can't, he's only six years old. Maybe when he's sixteen. But I can't wait that long. I might already be dead. I can't miss these years with him.

So this is our last night.

Yes.

They went upstairs. In bed in the dark they talked a little more. Addie was crying. He put his arm around her and held her.

We've had a good time, Louis said. You've made a great difference for me. I'm grateful. I appreciate it.

You're being cynical now.

I don't mean to be. I mean what I've said. You have been good for me. What more could anyone ask for? I'm a better person than I was before we got together. That's your doing.

Oh, you're still kind to me. Thank you, Louis.

They lay awake listening to the wind outside the house. At two in the morning Louis got up and went to the bathroom. When he came back to bed he said, You're still awake.

I can't sleep, she said.

At four he got up again and dressed and put his pajamas and toothbrush in the paper bag.

Are you leaving?

I thought I would.

It's still night for a few more hours.

I can't see any point in putting this off.

She started to weep again.

He walked downstairs and went home past the old trees and the houses all dark and strange at this hour. The sky was still dark and nothing was moving. No cars in the streets. In his own house, he lay in bed watching the east window for the first sign of daylight.

40

As the weather held that fall Louis often walked out at night past her house and looked at the light shining upstairs in her bedroom, her bedside lamp that he knew and the room with its big bed and dark wooden dresser and the bathroom located down the hall, and remembered everything about the room and the nights lying in the dark talking and the closeness of it all. Then one night he noticed her face appear at the window and he stopped, she made no gesture nor any sign that she was looking at him. But when he was home again she called him on the phone. You can't do that anymore.

Do what?

Walk past my house. I can't have it.

So it's come to that now. You're going to tell me what I can do and can't do. Even in my own neighborhood.

I can't have you walking by and my thinking that

you are. Or wondering if you are. I can't be imagining you're out in front of the house. I have to be physically shut off from you now.

I thought we were.

Not if you walk by the house at night.

So he never passed her familiar house again, in the night. Walking past in the day didn't matter. And the few times they happened to meet at the grocery store or on the street, they looked at each other and said hello but that was all.

41

On a bright day just after noon when she was downtown by herself, Addie slipped on the curb on Main Street and fell and reached out to catch herself but there was nothing to catch on to, and she lay in the street until some women and a couple of men came to help her.

Don't lift me, she said. Something's broken.

The one woman knelt beside her and one of the men folded his coat under her head. They stayed there with her until she was taken away. At the hospital they said that she had broken a hip and she asked them to call Gene. He came that same day and it was decided that she would do better at a hospital in Denver. So she left Holt in an ambulance with Gene following in his car.

Three days later Louis was at the bakery with the group of men he met occasionally. Dorlan Becker said, I guess you know about her.

What are you talking about?

I'm talking about Addie Moore.

What about Addie Moore?

She broke her hip. They took her to Denver.

Where in Denver?

I don't know. One of the hospitals.

Louis went home and called the hospitals until he located the one she'd been admitted to and he drove the following day to Denver and got there in the early evening. At the information desk they told him her room number and he took the elevator to the fourth floor and walked down the hall and found her room and then stood in the doorway. Gene and Jamie were sitting there talking to her.

When Addie saw Louis her eyes teared up.

Can I come in? he said.

No, don't you come in here, Gene said. You're not wanted here.

Please, Gene, just to say hello.

For five minutes, he said. No more.

Louis entered the room and stopped at the foot of the bed and Jamie came around and hugged him and Louis held him close.

How's old Bonny?

She can catch a ball now. She jumps up and catches it.

Good for her.

Let's go, Gene said. We're leaving. Mom, five minutes. That's it.

He and Jamie left the room.

Will you sit down? she said.

Louis moved one of the chairs closer and sat beside
her, then took her hand and kissed it.

Don't do that, she said. She drew her hand back.
This is just for now. Just for a moment. That's all we
have. She looked at his face. Who told you I was here?

The guy at the bakery. Can you imagine his turning
out to be a help to me. Are you all right?

I will be.

Will you let me help you?

No. Please. You have to leave. You can't stay long.
Nothing's changed.

But you need help.

I've already started physical therapy.

But you'll need help at home.

I'm not coming home.

What do you mean?

Gene has it all figured out. I'll move to Grand Junction into assisted living.

So you won't come back at all.

No.

Christ, Addie. I don't accept any of this. It's not like
you.

I can't help it. I have to keep to my family.

Let me be your family.

But what happens when you die?

Then you can go live with Gene and Jamie.

No. I have to do this while I'm still able to make the adjustment. I can't wait until I'm too old. I won't be able to change then or I might not even have the option. You have to leave now. And please don't come back. It's too hard.

He leaned over and kissed her on the mouth and kissed her eyes and then went out of the room and down the hallway to the elevator. There was a woman on the elevator, she looked at his face once and looked away.

42

One night she called him on her cell phone. She was sitting in a chair at her apartment. Will you talk to me?

There was a long silence.

Louis, are you there? she said.

I thought we weren't going to talk anymore.

I have to. I can't go on like this. It's worse than before we ever started.

What about Gene?

He doesn't have to know. We can talk on the phone at night.

Then this seems like sneaking. Like he said. Being secretive.

I don't care. I'm too lonely. I miss you too much. Won't you talk to me?

I miss you too, he said.

Where are you?

You mean where in the house?

Are you in your bedroom?

Yes, I've been reading. Is this some kind of phone sex?

It's just two old people talking in the dark, Addie said.

43

Addie said, Is this a good time?

Yes. I just came upstairs.

Well, I was just thinking about you. I was just wanting so much to talk to you.

Are you all right?

Jamie came over again today after he got out of school and we went around the block. Bonny was here too.

Did he have her on a leash?

He didn't need to, she said. Jamie said his father and mother have been arguing and yelling. I said, What do you do then? He said, I go to my bedroom.

Well. I can be glad for him that you're there, Louis said.

Addie said, What have you been doing today?

Nothing. I shoveled snow. I made a path up in your block.

Why?

I felt like it. The people renting your house came out to talk to me. They seem all right. But it's still your house. Ruth's house is still hers too.

I feel that way about it too.

Well. Things have changed.

I'm in bed, she said, here in my room. Did I say that already?

No. But I assumed you were.

You know that play in Denver will be coming up. Why don't you use the tickets and go.

I won't go without you.

You could take Holly.

I don't want to do that. Why don't you use them?

I won't go without you either, she said.

Then some strangers will sit there in our seats. They won't know anything about us.

Or why the seats became available.

And you still don't want me to call you. You don't want me to initiate these calls.

I'm afraid someone will be here in the room with me. I wouldn't be able to cover up.

It's like when we started. Like we're started out new again. With you being the one to begin it again. Except that we're careful now.

But we're continuing too. Aren't we, she said. We're

still talking. For as long as we can. For as long as it lasts.

What do you want to talk about tonight?

She looked out the window. She could see her reflection in the glass. And the dark behind it.

Dear, is it cold there tonight?

Acknowledgments

The author wishes to thank Gary Fisketjon, Nancy Stauffer, Gabrielle Brooks, Ruthie Reisner, Carol Carson, Sue Betz, Mark Spragg, Jerry Mitchell, Laura Hendrie, Peter Carey, Rodney Jones, Peter Brown, Betsy Burton, Mark and Kathy Haruf, Sorel, Mayla, Whitney, Charlene, Chaney, Michael, Amy, Justin, Charlie, Joel, Lilly, Jennifer, Henry, Destiny, CJ, Jason, Rachael, Sam, Jessica, Ethan, Caitlin, Hannah, Fred Rasmussen, Tom Thomas, Jim Elmore, Alberta Skaggs, Greg Schwipps, Mike Rosenwald, Jim Gill, Joey Hale, Brian Coley, Troy Gorman and most especially Cathy Haruf.